Singing from the Gallows:

The Story of "Bad Tom" Smith

Wayne Combs

Published by
AKA-Publishing
Columbia, MO 65203

AKA-Publishing.com

ISBN 978-1-936688-74-6 Trade Paper

ISBN 978-1-936688-75-3 eBook

Compass
Flower
Press

Compass Flower Press

an imprint of AKA Publishing

Singing From the Gallows

The Story of "Bad Tom" Smith

Wayne L. Combs

Contents

Dedication

This work is dedicated to my daughter Christin, who has two great-great-grandfathers mentioned in this book. One was as good as the other was bad.

Dedication

Acknowledgements

This book took years to write, and I want to thank those who have helped me in the process. My wife, Carol, did many hours of exhaustive research, and contributed greatly to the finished product. A special thanks to Robert Ludwig, who did the artwork for the cover and encouraged me to finally finish the book. Also, a thank you to Charles Hays, the publisher of *The Kentucky Explorer* magazine, for writing the forward to the book. Yolanda Ciolli of AKA-Publishing is responsible for the book getting into print under the Compass Flower Press imprint.

Foreword

I first read an account of Bad Tom Smith and the Fult French Gang published in our local newspaper, The Jackson Times, when I was still a student at Quicksand Grade School in the late 1950s. Years later, I came across more articles concerning Smith and his role in the famed French-Eversole War of Perry County and the fact he was the first and only man ever legally hanged in Breathitt County. These stories of feuds and outlaw days in Eastern Kentucky started me out in a career dealing with local and state history which has continued even to this day.

Back in 1969, I put together a small booklet recounting the life and times of Tom Smith, including an account of his hanging. The little book was well-received, and the 1,000 copies soon sold out. Now, some 44 years later, it is a real treat to learn of Wayne Combs' new book on Bad Tom called Singing From the Gallows. The wonderful details and a keen insight make his book not only a joy to read, but offers many facts not known by most of us. It is evident much research and hard work have gone into the composition.

To truly appreciate the story of Bad Tom Smith, we must remember the late 1800s as being a time of lawlessness and anarchy not only in Kentucky, but throughout America. Yet, few places suffered through this age of violence as did the highlands of Eastern Kentucky. For several generations the settlers had been cut off from mainstream America, and thus mountain society and customs were a throwback to a much earlier time. While it is true men were elected to uphold the law, in many cases the lawmen were either too weak or too crooked to enforce peace and order. This breakdown allowed for stronger forces to step in and, in some cases, take over whole towns. Clans and factions formed along family lines for financial reasons. Feuds and "wars" were a constant part of everyday life in the mountains of Kentucky from the 1860s until about 1912.

It was a time when family honor demanded revenge for the slightest insult. Often mountaineers took to the woods seeking out defenseless victims to be shot from ambush. In other cases, without proper schooling or any chance for success, many young mountain men found themselves hired to do the fighting and killing for wealthy and vengeful bosses. Tom Smith was one of these men. He seemingly hired his deadly gun out to the highest bidder in some cases, but in other instances he was just simply bad. According to his own confession made on the day he was hanged, June 28, 1895, he murdered several men and committed other foul deeds.

In the annals of local history, some men are almost bigger than legend. Such is the case of Tom Smith, a man who during his lifetime carried the name of "Bad Tom." In an age when murder and ambush were common, few bad men earned the title of "Bad," but the bloody deeds of Tom Smith more than justify his title. Even today, nearly

120 years after his hanging, when someone speaks of him, he is called Bad Tom Smith.

However, even the meanest man has a story to be told. He is not mean all the time. As the reader will soon learn, Tom Smith was not all bad. Wayne Combs does a masterful job of bringing out every facet of Bad Tom's life, both the good and bad. For the reader, there will be some interesting surprises along the way.

Charles Hayes
Owner/Publisher
Kentucky Explorer Magazine
Jackson, Kentucky

Introduction

In the spring, summer, and fall, southeastern Kentucky, the proud home of the Cumberland Mountain Range, is one of the most beautiful places on the earth. However, those Appalachian Mountains look bland and bleak in the winter. The numerous trees that cover the not very tall—but quite steep—mountains show us a breathtaking green from spring to autumn. In the fall, the leaves magically change to various shades of brown, gold, red, and yellow. For a week or so, the hills come alive with breathtaking beauty. Then the landscape looks barren and disrobed throughout the winter, with only a few pine trees and some scrub brush growing out of the snow, making the environment look depressing to many people in the cold winter. But with spring just around the corner, there is always hope for Kentucky's Cumberland Mountain people.

Hazard is the county seat of Perry County. In the Appalachian chain, Hazard is located in the middle of the Cumberlands. Because Hazard and Perry County number among the few "wet" places in southeastern Kentucky—meaning that liquor is sold legally there—Perry is one of the most prosperous mountain counties in the state. However, that affluence has come at a great price. Sometimes a great deal of violence takes place in the taverns and bars. "First Chance" and "Last Chance" beer joints seem to dot every county line crossing.

Perry County was formed in 1821 from portions of Floyd and Clay Counties thirty years after Kentucky, which had been called Kentucky County, Virginia, was taken away from the Old Dominion and admitted to the Union as the fifteenth state. Before Kentucky County became a state, it consisted of three Virginia counties— Jefferson, Fayette, and Lincoln. In 1824, Elijah Combs and his seven brothers established a post office in the small community on the banks of the North Fork of the Kentucky River. Mail carriers and others traveling from Prestonsburg in Floyd County to Manchester in Clay County found Hazard a good rest stop. Then, a subsequent county courthouse was named Perry Courthouse.

Some people think Hazard got its name from being a violent and "hazardous" place to live. Actually, the town and county were named for American naval hero Commodore Oliver Hazard Perry, who helped defeat the British fleet in the Battle of Lake Erie during the War of 1812, then became an Admiral. A group of eastern Kentucky mountaineers traveled north to fight against the British with Perry. Perry died in 1819, before the town and county were named in his honor. In 1821, Perry County became Kentucky's 68th county. However, it was not until June 20, 1854 that the legislative record regularly referred to the site as Hazard. Prior to that date the county seat was referred to as Perry Courthouse. The county name was sometimes spelled Hazzard.

I was born in Hazard, just twenty-three days after the bombing of Pearl Harbor. When five or six years old, I realized there was a relative that my parents were interested in knowing more about. They did not wish to discuss the matter in front of me, however, one day my father bought a local newspaper with a historical article entitled "The Hanging of Bad Tom Smith." Only then did I learn that this man, who had confessed to numerous homicides and hanged for murder, was my great-grandfather. Thomas Smith was the father of my father's mother, Matilda Smith Combs. All of the adults called her "Tildy." I simply called her Grandma. She married Robert "Blue Bob" Combs, and they had twelve children. There were so many Combs men named Bob that colors were added to their names to identify them. I lived with my grandparents, Matilda and Blue Bob Combs, for about six months when I was a teenager in the late 1950s, shortly after my mother died of cancer.

A few years earlier, I remember playing cowboys and Indians with my cousin, Paul Jones of Lotts Creek, at my grandmother's house. Several of the Combs families had come for Sunday dinner. Paul walked into the kitchen and asked, "Grandma, was your daddy, Bad Tom Smith, a good shot?"

Grandma looked startled. She walked from the coal cook stove to the table with a huge cast iron skillet without saying a word. That question had conjured up a bad memory. Being a very quiet woman, Grandma didn't want to talk about her father. She quickly gained composure. "Paul, get out of my way, I wouldn't want to spill this good gravy on you and the floor."

One of the few times my grandmother broke her silence about her father was with her daughter—and my aunt—Nancy. Aunt Nancy liked to sing. She was singing some old-time songs around the house one day when my grandmother admonished her to quit singing because it would only lead to trouble. Nancy could end up like her grandfather, who also had liked singing. Tom Smith, I learned, did not only like to sing, but is said to have written several songs. Tom sang the last song he wrote for a group of reporters on the day before his execution.

Bad Tom had six children. My grandmother was thirteen years old, and the baby, Edgar, a little less than a year and a half in 1895, when their father was executed. The other children were Bud, Maggie, John, and Cody.

Sometimes family members of people who have been executed feel ashamed. There's a story about a woman who was very prominent in her town's society. One day she decided to trace family roots. The woman hired a genealogy expert to put together the family tree. After much research, the expert told her he had disturbing news. The woman's great-uncle had been hanged for murder. The lady talked to the genealogy expert privately. The expert issued a written report that stated a great-uncle had died "when a platform he was standing on suddenly collapsed."

I don't believe that shame accounted for Bad Tom Smith's children's reluctance to discuss him. Certainly they were not proud of the fact. But more important, I believe, is that the emotional trauma they suffered from this event, as children, never left them.

So, who was this man named Bad Tom Smith, who rode on horseback and led an outlaw gang through the hills and hollows of southeastern Kentucky, and ended up at the end of a noose? My purpose in writing this book is to answer that question by examining not just his death, but the events that shaped his life up to that fateful day.

Smith-Combs Genealogy

Ancestors and Descendants of "Bad Tom" Smith and Emaline (Combs) Smith

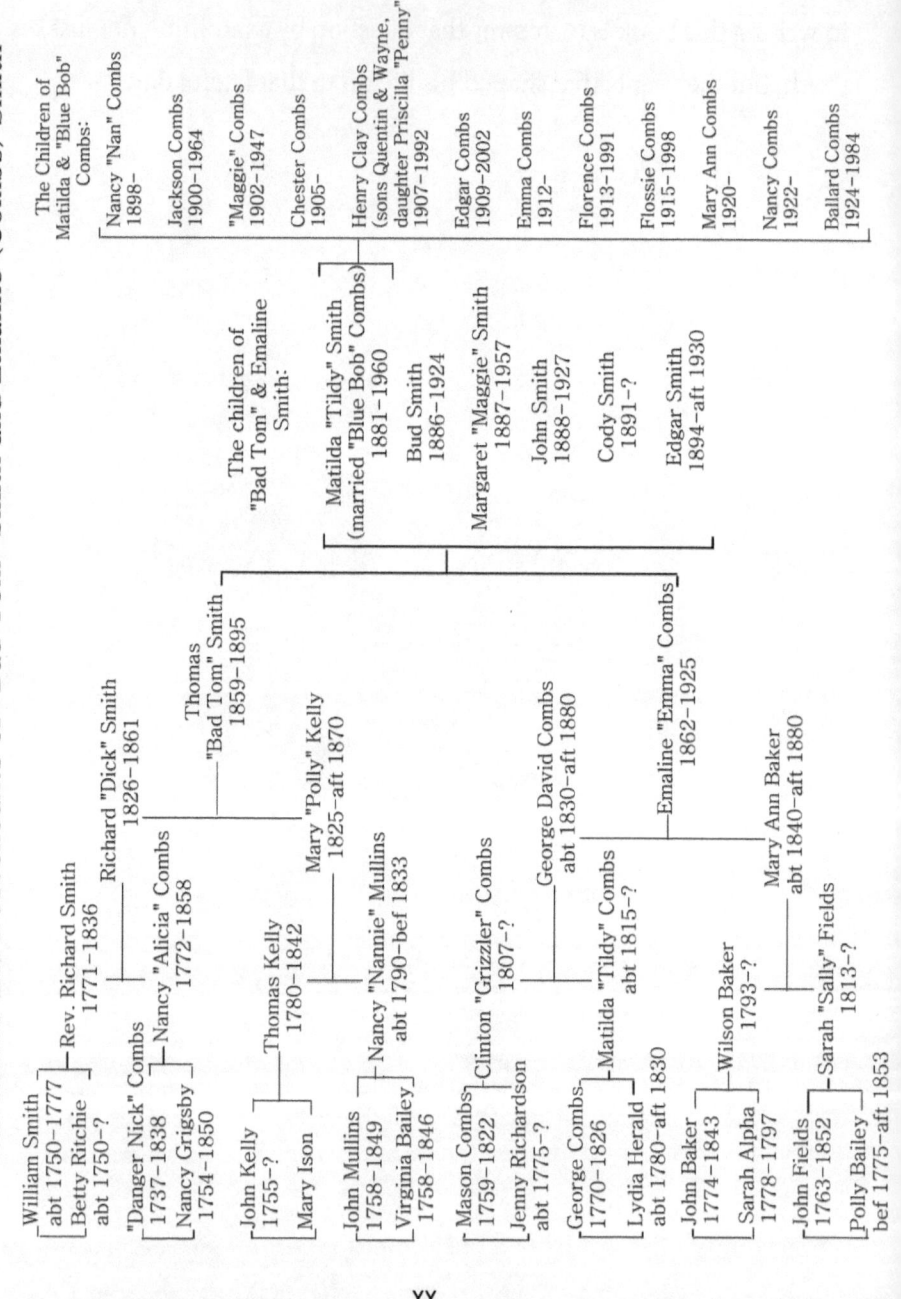

The Children of Matilda & "Blue Bob" Combs:

Nancy "Nan" Combs 1898–

Jackson Combs 1900–1964

"Maggie" Combs 1902–1947

Chester Combs 1905–

Henry Clay Combs (sons Quentin & Wayne, daughter Priscilla "Penny") 1907–1992

Edgar Combs 1909–2002

Emma Combs 1912–

Florence Combs 1913–1991

Flossie Combs 1915–1998

Mary Ann Combs 1920–

Nancy Combs 1922–

Ballard Combs 1924–1984

The children of "Bad Tom" & Emaline Smith:

Matilda "Tildy" Smith (married "Blue Bob" Combs) 1881–1960

Bud Smith 1886–1924

Margaret "Maggie" Smith 1887–1957

John Smith 1888–1927

Cody Smith 1891–?

Edgar Smith 1894–aft 1930

Thomas "Bad Tom" Smith 1859–1895

Emaline "Emma" Combs 1862–1925

Richard "Dick" Smith 1826–1861

Mary "Polly" Kelly 1825–aft 1870

George David Combs abt 1830–aft 1880

Mary Ann Baker abt 1840–aft 1880

William Smith abt 1750–1777

Rev. Richard Smith 1771–1836

Betty Ritchie abt 1750–?

"Danger Nick" Combs 1737–1838

Nancy "Alicia" Combs 1772–1858

Nancy Grigsby 1754–1850

John Kelly 1755–?

Thomas Kelly 1780–1842

Mary Ison

John Mullins 1758–1849

Nancy "Nannie" Mullins abt 1790–bef 1833

Virginia Bailey 1758–1846

Mason Combs 1759–1822

Clinton "Grizzler" Combs 1807–?

Jenny Richardson abt 1775–?

George Combs 1770–1826

Matilda "Tildy" Combs abt 1815–?

Lydia Herald abt 1780–aft 1830

John Baker 1774–1843

Wilson Baker 1793–?

Sarah Alpha 1778–1797

John Fields 1763–1852

Sarah "Sally" Fields 1813–?

Polly Bailey bef 1775–aft 1853

A Brief Historical Background of Some Mountain Characters and Characteristics

Tom Smith was born on October 13, 1859, in the tiny Perry County community of Carr's Fork, which would later become a part of Knott County after that county was formed from part of Perry County in 1885. Although Tom became an outlaw, he came from a respected family. William Smith was born in England and came to Virginia when it was still a colony in the eighteenth century. He married Betty "Eunice" Ritchie, also from England, shortly after arrival. Their son, Richard, was born March 6, 1771 in Virginia. After their father's death, Richard and his brother John moved to an unsettled part of Kentucky. Their mother stayed in Virginia to handle the plantations left by their father. Richard probably came to Owsley County, Kentucky by way of Pound Gap, Virginia in about 1792, along the route known as the Daniel Boone Trail. Richard then settled in the Lotts Creek area of Perry County before moving to Pigeon Roost, on Troublesome Creek, at Ary. According to Henry P. Scalf, in his book *Kentucky's Last Frontier*, Richard Smith owned 38,577 acres of land in 1796 through Eastern Land Titles. Richard was a Primitive Baptist Minister for forty-five years. He was said to preach hellfire and brimstone sermons, then sneak out back of the meeting place to take a swig of whiskey. According to Owsley County, Kentucky court records, Richard Smith's brother, John, was later appointed his guardian.

Richard Smith married Elita "Alicia" Combs in 1792, when she was twenty. Richard Smith, Jr. was the first of their fourteen children. He married Mary Polly Kelly and moved to the Carr's Fork area of what was then Perry County. The couple had eight children. Tom was the next to the last. His brother, Jeremiah, had died at only a year and a half. The patriarch of the family, Richard Smith, Jr., known as "Dick" to his family and friends, was killed at the Battle of Shiloh in 1862, less than three years after Tom's birth. Tom's mother, Mary Polly, had not been the same since receiving the news that her husband, a Union soldier, had been killed accidentally by his comrades in a "friendly fire" accident. Life had been hard as Mary Polly had no choice but to raise seven children by herself.

Hazard stretched up and down the North Fork of the Kentucky River. It was an isolated community. The natural barriers of the rugged Cumberland Mountains made traveling by wagon, mule, or horseback difficult. The railroad had not yet come to the craggy hill country. A decision had been made to extend the railroad to Jackson in Breathitt County, some thirty miles away, but that would be the end of the line.

Not many people traveled long distances in the Cumberland Mountains in the later part of the nineteenth century. However, those who did had no trouble finding accommodations. Hospitality was one of the virtues that mountain people both practiced and relied on. No matter how rich or poor a family was, it was a point of honor to offer shelter, food, and drink to any stranger that appeared at their door. This was a habit carried out by nearly all mountaineers. The practice is believed to have originated in the Scottish Highlands, where it is still in place today. Many of the mountain folk in Appalachia were descendents of the Scottish immigrants. When a friend or a stranger appeared at a cabin door, he could expect to receive the best the family could afford. A failure to accept a family's offer of hospitality was considered an insult.

Early Religion in Eastern Kentucky

During the lifetime of Bad Tom Smith, only a few scattered churches served all of the southeastern Appalachian area. Most of them were originally nondenominational, with few members. Religion did not loom large in the lives of most mountaineers, but they were willing to hear the sermons of any preacher who passed through, no matter what his doctrine. Most preachers were uneducated, barely literate, narrow-minded, and dogmatic. Many used rhythmically chanted preaching and urged congregational shouting. Some practiced foot washing and a few promoted snake handling. Most insisted on natural water—creek or river—baptism. Occasionally an educated preacher would hold a revival and attract large crowds. One of the first educated preachers to come into the eastern Kentucky mountains was Reverend George Owen Barnes. The Presbyterian Church had defrocked Reverend Barnes in 1866 for failure to wholeheartedly subscribe to the Westminster Confession. He was later accused of universalism. He became a self-supporting missionary to the mountain people of Kentucky. Not doctrinally rigid, the Reverend always gave his converts the choice of baptism by immersion or sprinkling. Barnes began his mountain ministry at Jackson, in Breathitt County, on November 12, 1879, pledging to preach "the true gospel." Jackson then consisted of a courthouse, twenty houses, and a mill. Barnes held a revival in the courthouse, during which he converted the county officials and the jail inmates. The incarcerated converts were baptized by immersion, then came out of the water to shake hands with the converted judge who had sentenced them. Deputy Sheriff Shade Combs brought a jail inmate charged with murder to the revival wearing handcuffs. The handcuffs were removed, and the jailer and the prisoner confessed their sins together. In all, there were 365 Jackson area residents converted. Reverend Barnes found Hyden, the county seat of Leslie County, the most unsympathetic mountain town in which he'd ever held a revival. Drunks brandished pistols, shooting right and left. Men walked restlessly in and out, constantly interrupting the services. One man walked up to the evangelist's daughter who was playing the organ, an object of curiosity to everyone. Taking out his pistol, he laid it on top of the instrument. Barnes's daughter, Marie, continued to play the organ while the man divided his attention between the preaching and the uproar outside. Sometimes the pistol fire outside increased in intensity, subsided, then got louder again. Suddenly, the man put his hand on the pistol as if to leave. Marie reached up, closed her hands over his on the pistol, and stared at him. He stared back for a moment, released the gun, and listened to the preaching. Reverend Barnes left Hyden for Hazard, grateful for his safety.

Hazard welcomed the clergyman with open arms. He preached at the courthouse to hospitable people who would not accept payment for lodging and refused to accept any money for items bought at the local stores.

Barnes left Hazard on July 14, 1880 headed for Whitesburg, in Letcher County. One of the people converted at a Reverend Barnes revival was Dr. Marshal Benton Taylor. Ten years later, Doc Taylor was involved in the infamous massacre of the Mullins Family at Pound Gap, Virginia. He was later hanged for the murders at what was then Gladesville, Virginia, and the execution was attended by author John Fox, Jr. During his work as an evangelist, Reverend Barnes is credited for 26,000 converts, with 20,000 of them in the mountains of eastern Kentucky.

Chapter 1

Attempted Escape

Tom Smith gave his sister a frightened and desperate look. "Millie, you gotta help me get out of here. They're gonna hang me! Them people mean it this time. You've got to help me get away!"

"Tom, what can I do? The jail is new and everybody says it's escape-proof. I'd help you if I could, but I just don't know what to do."

"I been thinking about that. Can you get me one of them small hacksaws and some blades to go with it? Those bastards put me in this cell so I would have to look at them building the gallows. If I could get a hacksaw and blades, I could get out of here. The last laugh would be on them."

"But Tom, how could I get something like that to you without them knowing it?"

"Hide the stuff in some food that you bring me. I think I can saw right through the bars."

"What kind of food?"

"You've already brought me food before. Fix me a big bowl of soup beans and bake me a pone of cornbread. Then, put the little saw and blades in the cornbread batter before you bake it. Bring the soup beans and the corn pone to me at the jail. The jailer won't suspect nothin'. He won't tear my cornbread apart."

"All right, Tom, I'll do it. I just hope I don't get caught."

"You won't, sis. You won't."

Millie Smith left the Breathitt County Jail in Jackson, where her brother was incarcerated for the murder of Dr. John E. Rader, a local physician. Millie didn't like the idea of helping Tom break out of jail, but she didn't want to see him hanged either. Millie was determined to do anything she could to help Tom.

A jury had found Tom Smith guilty of first degree murder in the doctor's death and recommended execution by hanging. The judge agreed. He pronounced the sentence, to be carried out May 31, 1895. An appeal had moved the execution date to June 28, 1895. Smith, known as Bad Tom Smith throughout the southeastern Kentucky mountain counties of Breathitt, Perry, Knott, and Letcher, had been in jail since his arrest shortly after the murder on February 25th of that year.

He had been charged with murder before, but through political influence and intimidation had managed to elude justice. This time was different. Smith believed they would go through with it. He was deathly afraid for one of the few times in his thirty-five years.

That night, after Millie's visit, he began to feel strange. Tom knew what was coming. It had happened before, but he could do nothing. Tom began to shake, then fell down on the cell floor. His body shook and he began to foam at the mouth and to howl in a long, deafening screech! The jailer noted in his record that at two o'clock in the morning, Tom Smith had a "fit" which woke all the jail's residents. The jailer and prisoners discussed what they had heard and reached differing conclusions. Some thought it was the result of Bad Tom's possession by demons. Others attributed his howling to a nightmare stemming from the unspeakable crimes he had committed.

Three days after the promise to smuggle a small hacksaw and blades into the jail for her brother, Millie Smith brought a big bowl of pinto beans and a freshly baked pone of cornbread to Tom. She approached the jailer, H.W. Centers. "Mr. Centers, Tom says he hain't had no soup beans and freshly baked corn pone since being in here. I fixed some. Is it all right if I give this to him?"

Centers took the bowl of beans to look at, and stirred them a little with a letter opener on his desk. He then looked at the pone of cornbread, felt the weight of it, and told Millie, "That looks good. Go ahead and give them to him. Let me unlock the cell door for you."

Millie took the beans and cornbread in to Tom and talked with him for a few minutes before leaving. She was nervous, afraid everyone would see her shaking. Feeling sure she would be found out, Millie's back began to sweat. Not one person in the jail paid any attention to her.

When no one was around, Tom tore the cornbread pone apart to retrieve a small hacksaw and six blades. The tray from lunch was still in the cell. He took the cloth napkin from it to wipe the gooey cornbread residue from the saw and blades. Tom found a hard cardboard tube on the cell's window sill. He placed the saw and blades inside the tube and put it back in the window. The tube had been there before he was placed in the cell, so no one would bother to inspect it.

Later that evening, after all the prisoners were asleep and the guard was dozing off, Tom began sawing on one of the bars. He did a little sawing each evening. Tom filled in the gaps on the bars with a mixture of soap and dirt obtained from the cell floor to hide the cuts. After each session, Tom placed the saw and blades back inside the tube on the window sill.

A week had gone by since Millie brought the cornbread. By sawing a little bit late each night, he had cut two bars on the window nearly in half. When Tom completed that, he would have just enough space to get his body through the window. The hanging was scheduled less than a month away, but just one more session with the hacksaw would make him a free man again. No hangman's noose for Bad Tom!

"H.W., have you got the supplies from the lumber company to build the gallows for Bad Tom yet?" Sheriff Breckinridge Combs asked the jailer as he walked into the jail. Combs was the Breathitt County Sheriff and was known by the nickname of "Wild Hog." He knew Bad Tom Smith well. Combs didn't like being the official responsible for the hanging of a man he considered a friend, a man who was also his second cousin. But it was his job and society demanded it.

"I talked to them today, Breck. They're supposed to deliver the lumber tomorrow. I've hired a couple of boys in town to build it."

"Good, H.W. I wish I could find a rope that easy. The only thing I can find around here is that little old one-inch stuff. You can't hang a man with that flimsy a rope. I telegraphed to Louisville, and they said they will try to find me some suitable rope. By the way, you don't think some of Bad Tom's former gang members might try to break him out of jail, do you?"

"No, our security is too good. And the jail itself is new. These cells are built solid. I don't think he can get out of here. I wouldn't worry about it."

"If you say so, H.W. It was just a thought, that's all. I heard that Bad Tom's brother Bill has been going around making threats. The word on the street is that Bill threatened to kill the four lawyers that testified against his brother. He said they had only four days to live."

"I wouldn't pay no attention to that, Breck. Bill is just shooting off his mouth. He never did have the nerve his younger brother does. The only time Bill had enough guts to do anything risky was when he was with Tom. He won't do nothin'. Now that French gang of Bad Tom's is another story. Joe Adkins is as mean as Bad Tom. They really might try something. That's why I have four guards stationed in the jail at all times. I also have some dynamite, and have given orders if any attempt is made to break Bad Tom Smith out of jail, then blow up his cell with him in it. Bad Tom is not going to get out, no matter what!"

"You know, H.W., this hanging is something I really don't want to do. Bad Tom is my second cousin and I remember when we were boys playing with each other at my parents' place on Old Quicksand Road. We spent a lot of time together, and they were the best times ever! I like Tom, and don't want to hang him, but it's my duty. That's what they elected me for."

After supper early one evening, another prisoner, Ike Montgomery, who was serving a short sentence, passed a note to the jailer. Centers unfolded the piece of paper and read it. It detailed Bad Tom's escape preparations. Montgomery's cell was adjacent to Smith's. He had heard Smith sawing the bars for the last few nights.

The jailer was skeptical. Montgomery was just having some fun, he thought. However, it was his responsibility to make sure. Centers rounded up two deputy sheriffs to accompany him. The jailer knew Smith had killed several men; he didn't want to be the next.

With the two deputies following, Centers went to Bad Tom's cell. Smith was seated in a wooden chair. "Smith, I want you to stay in that chair," the jailer warned.

"If you say so," Tom said.

"Tom, there's a rumor going around the jail that you're planning an escape. Is there anything to that?" the jailer asked.

"No sir," Bad Tom said. But Centers noticed that Smith, usually cool, seemed quite nervous. Something was wrong, the jailer knew.

"Boys, take this prisoner to the empty cell, the one with no windows," Centers said. The deputies then marched Bad Tom out of the cell and down the hallway to the windowless corner cell.

Centers ordered a search of Bad Tom's former cell. At first the inspection turned up nothing. After a few minutes, however, the jailer spotted the cardboard tube in the window. He opened it and found the small hacksaw and blades. A further examination revealed that two bars on the window were nearly sawed in half. He also spotted the soap and dirt mixture Smith had used to hide his handiwork. Centers decided to keep Smith in the windowless cell until the date with the hangman. Sheriff Combs concurred.

The following day, Tom's older brother, Bill, came to see him. He was thoroughly searched before being allowed to enter Tom's cell. "I heard about the jailer finding the saw and the cut bars, Tom. How did he find out?"

"I'm not sure. I think that bastard that was in the cell next to mine told him," Bad Tom said. "He must have heard me sawing. That man had better be glad I'm still in here. If I could, I'd kill the son of a bitch."

"What about Millie, Tom? Do they know she brought you the saw and blades?"

"They might suspect it was her but they can't prove it. Since I didn't escape, they won't do nothin'. Tell Millie I really appreciate what she did."

"Okay, Tom, I'll tell her."

"Bill, I don't know what I'm gonna do! I've been thinking about myself and I don't think I would have done all the things that I've done if it hadn't been for them damn fits. As you may remember, those fits started when I had just turned fourteen back on Carr's Fork."

Chapter 2

Young Tom

The warmth from the kitchen fireplace felt good this dreary, rainy, cool—almost cold—1873 day in the tiny Perry County community of Carr's Fork. The community would be located in Knott County after 1885. Mary Polly was partial to Tom. Something about him seemed different from the other children. She did not assign Tom as many chores as his four brothers and two sisters. The eldest boy in the family, Isaac, was <u>ten</u> years older than Tom. He became more like a father than a brother to Tom, Sam, Alexander, Bill and their sisters, Millie and Dulciney. However, Isaac lacked the authority their father had exercised, and thus he was not an effective disciplinarian. Mary Polly had always depended on her husband to discipline the children. She quickly discovered that—like Isaac—she lacked the skills to command respect for authority.

A typical farm day began at dawn. Although Tom strayed from the work ethic and eventually became an outlaw, the Smith children were known as hard workers. Mary Polly made sure that the boys—Isaac, Sam, Bill, Tom, and Alexander, headed out to the fields for an hour or two of work while she and her daughters, Millie and Dulciney, fetched fresh hen eggs and several forty pound pails of water, then "set" the bread (mixing the dough and letting it rise). Next, Mary Polly started breakfast. Depending on the season, she fixed sausage, bacon, or salt pork with gravy. Side dishes included fried eggs and fried Irish or sweet potatoes. Salt was the only commercial product cooks used regularly. Sugar was a luxury; mountain women made do with wild honey or sorghum molasses.

After breakfast, all seven children went into the fields. Mary Polly then began to prepare the noon meal—called "dinner"—the main meal of the day. "Supper"—the evening meal—usually consisted of cold leftovers. Sweet milk and buttermilk with leftover cornbread, eaten out of a glass or cup, might be a before-bedtime snack.

For the mountain people, a cheap source of meat was hogs. They would go out and root around in the woods for food. Therefore, the Smith family didn't have to feed pigs much. A few cattle were kept. There was always a milk cow or two. Families and neighbors would take turns having a beef slaughtered, and divide the meat among themselves before it spoiled. Also, the families preserved meat for winter by salting or smoking. Wild game like deer, rabbits and squirrels, freshly caught fish, and dry land fish (morel mushrooms) were important supplements in those days as well. The chickens provided eggs, meat, and feathers for pillows and featherbeds (homemade mattress covers stuffed with feathers).

As for vegetables, there was no canning. Some vegetables like cabbage and green beans were pickled in stoneware crocks. Fruits and green beans were often dried for the wintertime. In mid-July at berry picking time, Bill Smith would pick as much as thirteen and a half quarts of blackberries by himself in a day. Tom could pick a respectable amount, but only if he chose. Always trying to pick a few more berries than his sister, Millie, Tom believed it didn't look good for a girl to out-pick him.

Tom discovered early on that he liked to kill things. One day while out picking blackberries, Tom killed a five foot rattlesnake with sixteen rattles on its tail.

Tom was named after Thomas Kelly, his mother's brother. Kelly was an "Old Regular" Baptist minister. He taught all the Smith boys how to handle a gun. Kelly noticed that Tom had a special talent with firearms. He told Mary Polly, "You know Tom favors the Kelly side of the family."

Kelly started taking Tom out in the woods when he was only eight years old, showing him how to use both a pistol and a rifle. The first time he fired a weapon, the boy could hardly stand up to the jolt. But after Tom grew accustomed to it, he could fire both weapons steadily. By ten, little Tom could hit a target fifty feet away with ease. In his early teens, he continued to shoot in the forest by himself, becoming one of the best marksmen in the area. Tom often supplied the family with rabbit, squirrel, and other small game killed in the woods.

During his excursions into the woods, Tom often carried a small tablet and wrote song lyrics. Then, he figured out tunes. One of his acquaintances taught him how to play the banjo. In the forest, the boy sang his own songs and accompanied himself. After singing a concert, Tom sometimes took a bow and then shook hands with the tree branches.

African-American musicians introduced the first banjos to North America as early as the seventeenth century. They made them from gourds, with a stick neck and strings. Tom Smith's banjo was the traditional type we would recognize today. After numerous solo concerts in the woods, Tom finally began singing some of his songs at home. Word spread in the hollows that Tom was a good singer, and he began to be asked to sing before groups at social gatherings and occasionally at church services. At the age of fourteen, an incident occurred that forever changed his life. One afternoon, <u>Mary</u> Polly took a big iron pot of bubbling milk gravy off the kitchen fire and began pouring it into a bowl on the round oak table top. Then, suddenly, Tom fell at her feet. He gagged, then yelled. His entire body shook and his head banged the floor.

"You nearly made me spill this good gravy!" Mary Polly screamed.

"I'm sorry Ma, something just come over me all of a sudden," Tom said weakly.

He pulled himself up using the table leg, without help from his mother. That was the first of Tom's "fits." As they continued, and got worse, his mother took him into the village of Hindman to see the doctor. The physician did not know how to treat the problem. In the next few months, Tom saw several doctors, going as far as Hazard and Whitesburg. None of them could help. The fits grew worse, forcing Tom to behave strangely. At this point, some people in the community began calling him "Bad Tom" Smith.

Tom became a frequent topic of conversation among the men in the little village as they sat around the big black pot-bellied stove at the combination general store and post office. Once, Clyde Campbell, whittling on a piece of wood, looked over at Joe Sexton and said, "Have you seed that Smith boy? He's a biggun, hain't he? When Tom has one of them fits of his'n, he scares the hell out of me!"

"Clyde, we gotta do something about that boy. He's full of the devil, that's what he is! We gotta run him outta here."

"No, Joe. The only way we're gonna get shed of that boy is to kill him. We oughta go strang him up on the nearest tree. We don't want no devil round here!"

Many residents of the Carr's Fork area suggested that something ought to be done about Tom Smith. None of the threats were ever carried out, however.

One summer morning, Mary Polly told Tom, "I need some salt, flour, and corn meal. Tell Mr. Amburgy I don't have no money today, but I'll pay him next month. He knows I'm good for it."

"Okay ma. I'm on my way."

Tom was halfway to the country store and post office on Carr's Fork, a distance of a couple miles, when he met two boys of about his age, John Napier and Cletus Couch. "Howdy," Tom said.

"Cletus, did you hear that? The crazy boy can talk."

"Yeah, John, I thought maybe Tom had bit off his tongue during one of his fits. He shore does everything else when having a fit. Tom rolls over, shakes, screams, and hollers. Why don't you show us one of your fits, crazy boy?"

Embarrassed and angry, Tom turned red in the face. "Cletus Couch, I'll show you something all right, and hit won't be no fit. Hit'll be a fist!"

Without further warning, Tom hit Couch on the chin and knocked him down. Napier swung at Tom and missed. Tom smashed his fist into Napier's stomach, doubling him over. Tom pulled Napier up and slammed his head into Couch's. He then proceeded toward the store.

While Tom's fits did not win any popularity in the tiny community, size and athleticism protected him. Many of the other young people in Carr's Fork made fun, teased, and called the boy names behind his back, but few dared to do it to his face or take him on physically. Those who did attempt to tangle, like John Napier and Cletus Couch, regretted it.

Tom's mother eventually learned how to help her son when his fits came on. She held his head, making sure he didn't swallow his tongue. Then she sang some of his favorite hymns, which always had a calming effect. Soon the fits became less of a hazard. However, they had already made the boy an outcast and a loner.

Like many other mountain children, Tom did not attend school. However, an educated man in the community, called "Professor" Billy Thomas, took an interest in Tom and taught him to read, write, and solve some basic arithmetic problems.

One day Professor Thomas decided to go beyond the basics. He asked Tom, "Do you know who the king of the United States is?"

Tom stood up and said, "There hain't no sechie thing as a king in the United States. We have presidents."

Professor Thomas at first looked pleased by Tom's answer, but then frowned. "That's right Tom, but I thought I learned you better

Anglish than that. Don't you know there hain't no sechie word as sechie?"

Young Tom's social unacceptability in the community led to long periods of solitude. However, the writing continued. In his early teens, he spent hours by himself, using a pencil and tablet to write ballads.

Tom did appreciate the communal nature of church services, however. He always had a nice voice, and joining in the congregational singing was his favorite part. The melody and the way the words flowed together made him feel better. His mother never had to force him to go to the occasional church service on Sunday. He looked forward to it..

At church, Tom was exposed to the Ten Commandments. However, they did not make much of an impression. After he began suffering the fits and became a social outcast, Tom started stealing anything not nailed down. He started by taking the pocket knives of his companions. Tom stole watermelons, roasting ears, fruit, and other produce from neighborhood gardens. He once stole a trout line and all the attached hooks from the North Fork of the Kentucky River. For the next few years of his life, Tom learned the arts of stealing and burglary through on-the-job training.

Chapter 3

The French-Eversole Friendship

As Tom was growing into maturity and beginning to acquire criminal habits, a relationship between two men he did not know—but whose futures would profoundly affect his—had begun to develop, along with the economy of Perry County.

In 1886, logging was Hazard's only industry, other than a few small hillside farms. Loggers cut the trees and floated the logs down the North Fork into the main Kentucky River, then to the flat Bluegrass area. This remained a small-scale operation until 1912, when the railroad came to Perry County and Hazard.

Another extractive industry developed even more slowly. Early in the eighteenth century, Christopher Gist, one of the Cumberland Mountains' earliest explorers, reported discovering bituminous coal in the area. Several decades later, geologists determined its extent and quality.

The state of Kentucky sent explorers to the area as early as 1836. They found that the seams were extensive and of a high grade for bituminous coal. The scientific and industrial communities had known about Kentucky's mineral riches for several decades. However, the mountain people who lived there were largely ignorant of it. What little they did know about coal came about by accident. In 1877, a forest fire ignited a coal seam on King's Creek in Letcher County. People from throughout the area traveled there to marvel at the burning earth. In this way they discovered that the black rock they occasionally came across would burn.

Nearly all the people in the mountains of Kentucky burned wood as a fuel. Most did not know about coal. However, a few of the Perry County mountaineers who had witnessed the King's Creek fire began to occasionally dig a hundred bushels or so of coal and float it down the Kentucky River on rafts or flatboats to sell at Frankfort or Richmond.

The fortunes of Ballard Fulton French and Joseph Castle Eversole would grow with the developing economy of the mountain area. Both were respected lawyers. Eversole was small and wiry, no more than five feet five inches tall. He always wore the latest style suits and ties. His family had been among the earliest settlers of the area. He had numerous relatives in Perry and surrounding counties. Eversole was a Mason and a Republican, involved in GOP politics at the national level. He served as a delegate to the 1884 GOP convention held at Exposition Hall in Chicago, representing Kentucky's tenth district. This presented a distinct honor for a young backwoods lawyer and merchant.

Fulton "Fult" French measured nearly six feet. Like Eversole, he always wore a suit and tie in public. He had come to Kentucky from North Carolina. French first settled on Cutshin Creek in what is now Leslie County. Although French was not a native of Kentucky, his wife, the former Mary Jane Lewis (who was known as Lillie), was born and raised at Cutshin. Through marriage, French was related to some prominent families in the surrounding counties of Leslie and Breathitt. He moved to Hazard in Perry County in 1874, and for a while taught school. Fult "read" law, as was the habit in that era, and then opened a practice. He soon ran for Perry County Attorney, and won. Eversole hired him to clerk part-time in his store. The two attorneys became fast friends. Both wanted to bring economic development to Hazard.

One fine day in 1881, Joe Eversole appreciated the beauty of the mountains as he carefully walked across Main Street—trying hard to avoid piles of fresh horse manure—but his mind was on more practical matters. His business, like those of other prominent citizens, was not what it should be. Hazard needed jobs. The local logging businesses employed only a handful of men. In order to thrive, Hazard would have to create many more jobs.

Land containing known coal reserves and mineral rights was selling quickly in Breathitt County in anticipation of the coming of the railroad. Perry County had huge coal reserves—probably greater than Breathitt—but without the railroad, there was no way to haul it out. And there were no plans to extend the railroad to Hazard. Eversole conceded that he had more than the community's benefit on his mind. People with jobs would spend their wages in his store.

Eversole's reverie abruptly ended when his newly shined black high-top shoe sank down nearly to the top in a pile of rain-dampened horse manure. He mumbled a few profanities, then gingerly walked across the street, trying to avoid stepping into another pile.

Eversole stopped at the edge of the wooden sidewalk on the other side of Main Street to scrape the manure off. He then walked into his store.

"Fult, you know this town needs the railroad, needs it bad. We should get Kentucky Union to run their tracks from Jackson on in to Hazard."

"I'm with you there, Joe. Let's get our businessmen together and go see the rail company." He paused. "Hey. You going to be at the school board meeting tonight?"

"Glad you reminded me. I'd plum forgot. What time is it gonna be?" Eversole said.

"I've got seven o'clock written down on the calendar."

Eversole walked to the door. "See you tonight, then."

Both men were members of the school board. They had tried to expand the school year, but that was a hard sell in an agricultural community. Perry County schools began classes in July and they ran for about four months. Never high, school attendance dwindled to next to nothing at "fodder pulling" time. Eversole and French knew that expanding the school year to perhaps as much as nine months would not work until the fathers of the children had jobs beyond logging and hillside farming, both of which required labor of the children. The men believed that a combination of the railroad and the vast coal resources of Perry County offered the best answer.

For nearly seventy years after the state of Kentucky was established from part of Virginia, most of it had no school system at all. There was virtually no education of even the simplest form in the mountains of

Kentucky until after the Civil War. Some of the scattered mountain communities made efforts to teach children how to read and write. Tom Smith and the children in his small area learned some fundamentals of reading and writing, usually from relatives who had managed to obtain some degree of primitive education.

When Eversole arrived for the school board meeting at the town's one-room schoolhouse, he noticed a boy waiting. "What can I do for you, son?" The boy appeared to still be in his teens, and was about six feet tall. He was not wearing a suit and tie, but was dressed better than most boys his age.

"I'm Dan F. Hamilton. I'm sixteen years old, and I want to be a teacher," the boy said.

"Son, you have to pass a test to be a teacher. You look too young to me."

"I'm not as old as the other teachers, but I've already passed the test. I took it yesterday. The school up on Cutshin Creek says they'll let me teach if you'll give me a certificate."

About that time Fult French walked up.

"Fult, this is Dan F. Hamilton. He's only sixteen, but they want him to teach up on Cutshin."

French looked at the boy. "Let me see your examination papers."

Hamilton turned over his credentials. French looked them over. "You've got nearly a perfect score. Where have you been studying?"

Hamilton looked at both men. "I've been staying with my half brother, John Hamilton, in Virginia, reading every book I could get my hands on."

French asked, "Are you the boy they say is Alexander Hamilton's great-great-grandson?"

"My folks tell me that Alexander Hamilton was my great-great-granddaddy."

Eversole looked at French. "Fult, let's sign the certificate. We could learn a thing or two from this boy! If young Dan was down in the Bluegrass, he'd really go places."

The two men, and another school board member who was also named Eversole (Harry), signed the teaching certificate and gave it to the teenager. Following the meeting, French and Joe Eversole walked out together.

"Joe, I've been thinking about our discussion about the railroad. I think we should go, just you and me, and try to convince the bigwigs to extend the railroad from Jackson to Hazard."

"I know of at least two men who would go into the coal business if the railroad was in Hazard," Eversole said.

"I'll contact the railroad office in Clay City to set up a time we can meet with them if you'll go with me."

"Sure, Fult. Maybe we can do some good."

The next day French sent a telegram to the Kentucky Union Railroad office in Clay City, requesting a meeting between himself, Joe Eversole, and an executive in charge of expansion. In a few hours the railroad sent a reply. The telegraph operator delivered the return telegram to Eversole's store.

French thanked the employee who delivered the telegram, then read it aloud. "'Mr. Fulton French, Hazard, Kentucky, stop. In regards to your request for a meeting to discuss expansion of our railroad from Jackson to Hazard, I would be happy to meet with you and Mr. Eversole next Wednesday at 1 PM at our Clay City office, stop. Reply if the date and time are agreeable, stop.' Signed: George W. Sewell, Land Agent, Kentucky Union Railroad."

French put the telegram in his breast pocket and walked across the dusty street to Eversole's law office. "Joe, I just got a reply from my telegram this morning. A Mr. Sewell will meet with us next Wednesday in his office in Clay City."

"That's great Fult. I'll be ready," Joe said.

"Joe, I was thinking. It might do some good if we circulated a petition around town asking the railroad to expand to Hazard. If we got a lot of signatures, it might impress the Kentucky Union folks."

"Hey, Fult, great idea! I'll go in right now and write one up. We'll start circulating it. I bet nearly everyone in Hazard will sign it."

French looked outside the door, and then at Eversole. "A lot of folks out in the county who come in here to buy their goods will sign it, too. Go ahead and put the petition together."

After French left his office, Eversole approached his oak roll top desk, got out a pen and some paper, and began writing. He wrote at the top of a piece of paper, in a precise, legible hand, "We the citizens of Perry County, Kentucky, beseech the Kentucky Union Railroad to expand its tracks from Jackson to Hazard. We, the undersigned, will cooperate in every way possible to achieve this expansion."

That left a generous amount of space for signatures. Eversole took the document, told his clerk he would be back shortly, and crossed the street to the store to show French the petition. They placed the first signatures on the document.

The only trouble French and Eversole had collecting signatures was that a large number of people in Perry County could not read and write. In many instances, people agreed to have someone write their name and then place their own "X."

The Kentucky Union had established headquarters at Clay City because it was a collection point for logs floated down the Red River. By the 1880s, the lumber industry was operating on a large scale and the Red River Lumber Mill, owned by Kentucky Union, was one of the largest steam-powered sawmills in the nation. However, by 1910 the timber supply was depleted and Clay City's economic growth had slowed.

Because they needed three days for travel, French and Eversole decided to leave for Clay City on Sunday, two days before the meeting. The two planned to ride the thirty miles to Jackson on horseback, stay all night, then ride on to Winchester, where they would spend the next night. The two men could catch the train into Clay City early Wednesday morning.

Fult French got up at five in the morning on Sunday, an hour earlier than usual. He had packed a tapestry bag the night before. Fult had to pack light because for most of the journey they would be on horseback, riding over several mountains. Fult's wife, Lillie, got up while he was putting on clothes. She went to the kitchen, opened the damper in the stove, then stirred the fire until it was blazing. Lillie put on a pot of coffee. Fult had told her the night before not to fix any breakfast, but she knew a cup of good hot coffee would take off some of the morning chill of the mountains. If Fult got hungry later he could eat some of the beef jerky placed in his bag.

"Honey, I'm ready to go."

"You and Joe be careful now. Watch out for snakes."

Fult walked to the barn, where he saddled up the horse and tied his bag securely to the saddle. Fult rode to the front door to say goodbye to Lillie, then took off for the big oak tree on the north end of Hazard where he was scheduled to meet Joe Eversole at 6:30.

Eversole wasn't there. Fult dismounted, tied the horse to a shrub, and sat leaning against the tree. French thought, it's early, only 6:20. Joe will be here in a few minutes.

Soon, Fult looked at his big gold ornamental pocket watch. "It is already 6:35. Did he forget the time? Has Joe changed his mind?"

Finally at 6:40, according to his watch, he heard hooves. Fult saw Joe Eversole riding toward him.

"Sorry, Fult. Five o'clock is a little too early for that old rooster of mine. I just overslept."

Fult mounted his horse, and the two rode off toward Jackson. The sun was just coming up, transforming the inky sky to a steel gray, then a slate blue. By the time they crossed the Perry County line, the sun was peeping through the slits in the lingering clouds. As they rode by creeks, ponds, and some open meadows, patches of fog took on the appearance of sleeping giants. Fult and Joe talked over the presentation they would make to George W. Sewell in Clay City. Their conversation was interrupted several times when the men had to ford streams on the road to Jackson. The "road" was not much wider than a wagon. Wheel ruts cut through the heavily forested hills. Sometimes the road seemed to disappear altogether. Occasionally the men found a spring in the side of a mountain and stopped for a drink of cool, clear water.

They stopped at a clearing at midday to eat some of the beef jerky and biscuits, following their snack with a healthy swig of moonshine that Fult had put in his canteen. Fult looked at Joe. "How much farther we got to go?"

"I figger we got another ten miles. We're more than halfway there."

French and Eversole reached Jackson late that afternoon. After an uneventful first leg of their journey, they needed a place to stay for the night before getting back on their horses the next day to head for Winchester.

Fult and Joe got off the horses in front of the Day Brothers' Store. They tied the animals up at the hitching post and then walked inside. "Do you have a hotel in this town?" Fult asked the clerk.

"Yes sir, we do. The Riverside Hotel is on the other side of the street, just a little bit further down. You can't miss it."

"Thank you," French replied. "Do you carry chewing tobacco?"

"Yeah, what kind you want?"

"I like that twist kind."

"Here it is. That's two cents."

Upon finding the hotel, they walked back across the street, got their horses, and took them to the livery stable they had spotted across from the hotel. The men paid for one night's room and board for their horses, then walked across to the Riverside Hotel and checked in.

Jackson had the reputation of being a wild town where you could get anything and nearly everything was legal. This held some appeal for Fult and Joe, but both were unused to long horseback rides and were bone tired. After supper at a restaurant close to the hotel, both men decided to go to bed early in preparation for more time in the saddle the next day.

French and Eversole didn't wake up until seven o'clock the next morning. After visiting the hotel outhouse and washing their hands, they were ready for breakfast. The men went back to the restaurant near the hotel. Both ordered two eggs sunny-side up, sausage, biscuits, and coffee. The waitress also brought some blackberry jam and butter. After paying for the breakfast, Fult and Joe decided to walk around town a bit before getting their horses from the livery stable to continue their journey.

The trip from Jackson to Winchester was much easier, as the terrain began to flatten out. They stopped three times along the trail—once to eat some more beef jerky, and twice to relieve themselves behind the nearest tree.

It was close to five PM before they trotted into Winchester, an even larger, more modern-looking town than Jackson. They quickly located a livery stable for their horses and a hotel for themselves. After checking in, they found a restaurant and quickly consumed an evening meal. They were bone tired and decided to go to bed early.

The next morning Joe and Fult again ate hearty breakfasts, then went to the train station to buy tickets.

"Fult, do you realize after we board that train we will make it to Clay City in less than an hour? Now that's moving on!"

"I know Joe, that's why we have to convince that Sewell feller to expand the railroad from Jackson to Hazard. With the railroad, Hazard could be the most important town in eastern Kentucky."

Joe and Fult arrived at the Winchester train depot about fifteen minutes before the train was scheduled to leave. Both carried only their tapestry bags with a few clothes. When the train pulled into the station with the locomotive belching a stream of black, sooty smoke from its stack, both Joe and Fult were impressed.

Joe, grinning from ear to ear, looked over at Fult. "I tell you, this is what we have to have in Hazard."

"We're gonna get it too, Joe," Fult said as they stepped—one at a time—on the stool the conductor had placed in front of the steps of the boarding car. Both walked through the first car into a larger lounge car where they found two empty seats. The train pulled away.

Fult and Joe sank down in their seats and relaxed as they looked out on the Bluegrass Country. Riding to Winchester on horseback, they had seen signs of a hardscrabble life, including an occasional shotgun shack with a group of rag-tag children playing in the front yard. It was obvious the flatlands they were now passing through were not nearly as poor. In his mind, Fult started reviewing his presentation to George W. Sewell in Clay City. All of a sudden, he heard a guitar strumming and somebody singing *Froggy Went a Courtin'.* Fult looked up and noticed a young man with blonde hair and a scrubby beard wearing dirty, rough-looking clothes. He strummed his guitar as he sang. Fult thought to himself, this boy ain't that bad. He introduced himself. "I'm Fult French from Hazard, and who would you be?"

The young man quit singing. "I'm Jeff Gabbard, from Winchester, or I used to be from Winchester. It don't seem like I have no home now. I just got out of jail back there. The sheriff accused me of breaking into some stores, but didn't have no proof. He bought me a train ticket and said to get out of town and not come back."

"That's too bad, son," Fult told Gabbard. "I really do like your singing. Pick and sing some more for us." Gabbard entertained the lounge car passengers all the way to Clay City.

French and Eversole got off the train and spotted a hotel across the street from the depot. They walked over and checked in. Fult and Joe went to their room, put their tapestry bags on a table, poured some water from the pitcher into the wash bowl, washed their hands, and swabbed the dust off their faces. They found a restaurant and then, after a hearty meal, decided to have some fun at the nearest saloon.

They got so drunk that they had trouble finding their hotel. The men didn't get into bed until after midnight. In the morning, French and Eversole felt as if little men with hammers were pounding on each side of their heads. They did not eat much for breakfast.

The meeting with George W. Sewell was scheduled for one o'clock that afternoon, thus giving them some time on their hands. They

27

decided to go shopping for presents for their wives. Both wanted to get something that their wives could not find in a backwoods town like Hazard. Fult found a small gold jewelry box for his wife; Joe bought his spouse a gold letter opener.

They arrived at the Kentucky Union offices about five minutes before one. George W. Sewell invited them into his office at precisely one PM. "Welcome to Clay City, gentlemen. I hope you had a pleasant journey."

"Yes we did, Mr. Sewell," Joe said to the railroad executive.

"Gentlemen, have a seat and let's hear what's on your mind," Sewell said as he pointed out two chairs in front of his massive mahogany desk.

Joe looked Sewell right in the eye. "Mr. Sewell, you know why we have come. Hazard is a backwoods town, but it has some very industrious people and rich coal reserves. The town needs the railroad, and the railroad could make a handsome profit by hauling coal to factories and other industries that need a constant and cheap source of power. We would like to see the Kentucky Union Railroad commit to expanding its tracks to Jackson and then on to Hazard. We have a petition here signed by fifty people in our county requesting that the railroad expand to Hazard."

"We would like your company to not only give us a commitment to expand, but also a timetable as to when we can expect the first train in Hazard," Fult chimed in before Sewell had a chance to respond.

"Gentlemen, I commend your civic pride in coming here today, but I'm afraid I cannot give you such a commitment."

"Why not?" Joe asked.

"Well, it costs a lot of money to build railroad tracks in the mountains. Digging tunnels and building bridges are terribly expensive ventures."

Sewell said the company would expand to Hazard and beyond, but not right now. He said the original plan for the railroad was for tracks to run from either Covington or Newport in northern Kentucky, through central Kentucky and Lexington, and on through Powell, Breathitt, Perry, and Letcher counties to Cumberland Gap, and to Big Stone Gap, Virginia, where it would connect with the Virginia and Tennessee Railroad. Sewell added that getting it just to Jackson was going to be expensive enough. He added that the cost for the railroad was forty thousand dollars a mile to lay the track. "We decided to expand to Jackson to see if it is feasible to open up the eastern part of Kentucky, but our timetable for the first train to Jackson is not until 1891. Then, we will need time to evaluate whether that large investment is worth the cost. If the railroad finds that it is a good investment, we will certainly consider going into Hazard and even beyond, but I'm afraid that will be years away."

"Hazard and Perry County are much richer in coal reserves than Jackson and Breathitt County. I don't understand why your plans don't already include us," Fult said.

"Unfortunately for your town gentlemen, Jackson is much closer to where the railroad tracks now exist, making an expansion there economically feasible," Sewell said. "I'm sorry I can't help you now. Perhaps in a few years."

29

Fult and Joe thanked Sewell for his time and left. "You know they can pay back an expansion investment very quickly in coal hauling fees. That company is too conservative. Their position is unrealistic," Joe said as the two stepped onto the street outside Sewell's office.

"I know, Joe. It's going to be a while before we get the railroad." They said little on the return trip. Both were deep in their own thoughts.

As it turned out, the Kentucky Union Railroad never reached Hazard. Not long after French and Eversole's meeting, the Kentucky Union Railroad found itself in financial trouble. F.D. Carley of Louisville, and others, issued three million dollars in gold bonds in 1888, and one million, three hundred thousand dollars in second mortgage gold bonds to finish the railroad into Jackson and to purchase new locomotives and rolling stock in 1890. The final three-mile stretch of track was laid beyond Jackson. In 1891, Kentucky Union defaulted on its obligations and went into receivership.

The Lexington and Eastern Railroad, organized in 1894, assumed operation of the Kentucky Union Railroad. In so doing, railroad management benefited from convict lease labor from the State Penitentiary in Frankfort. Kentucky Union frequently used this cheap source of labor in constructing tracks, tunnels, bridges, and numerous cemeteries along its route. The cemeteries, especially those near tunnels, contained as many as sixty bodies of men killed during construction.

Excursions to Natural Bridge became popular. A round trip from Lexington to Natural Bridge cost a dollar. The Lexington and

Eastern Route stretched from Winchester to Jackson. Its tracks passed through Clay City, Stanton, Natural Bridge (also known as McCormick's), Torrent, Fincastle, St. Helens, Tallega, Athol, and Elkatawa. The rail line to Natural Bridge and Torrent was completed around 1889, then extended into Jackson in the early 1890s. The Lexington and Eastern never reached Hazard. In November, 1910, the Louisville and Nashville Railroad took control of the shares of the Lexington and Eastern. Because of the unpopularity of the L&N at the time, the parties kept this deal secret for five years. The first L&N train finally rolled into Hazard on June 17, 1912.

When the Louisville and Nashville Railroad bought the Lexington and Eastern, it straightened curves along the line and reduced the grades so that larger and more powerful engines could haul coal from eastern Kentucky.

Chapter 4

French - Eversole Feud Begins

Six months had passed since Fult French and Joe Eversole's trip to Clay City. They remained friends, seeing each other at Eversole's store, at school board meetings, and at other functions. Each had a separate circle of friends. French became close to Silas Gayhart and to Bill Gambrill, whose family had been involved in a dispute with the Eversoles that had originated during the Civil War.

Before Kentucky became a state in 1789, Jacob and Mary Eversole moved to the present site of Krypton, now in Perry County, and built a one-room log cabin with a dirt floor. In 1800, Jacob Eversole enlarged the small cabin, converting it into a large two -story house featuring a middle walkway that people then called a "dogtrot." The house is still in existence today. At least one authority claims that the 1789 Eversole house was the first settlement in the mountains of eastern Kentucky. The old Eversole log structure became the home for several early eastern Kentucky families, including the children of Woolery Eversole and Lucy Cornett. Their son, John C. Eversole, born in 1828, became a major with the Union 14th Cavalry during the Civil War. His brother, Joseph, born in 1817, served in the Union War Commission Department. In 1849, Joseph Eversole served in the Kentucky Legislature.

During the Civil War, at least two major skirmishes occurred at the Eversole house. The first came at dawn one morning in 1862. About a hundred Confederate soldiers surrounded it. Union Major John C. Eversole and some of his men were inside. The Confederate soldiers were aware of that fact. They opened fire, breaking the windows and putting holes through the doors. The Union forces fled the house, crossed the river, and ran into the woods. Once behind the cover of trees and bushes, the Yankees returned fire, killing at least one Confederate. The rebel casualty was believed to be from the Gambrill family. The Eversoles all survived this firefight.

The Eversoles did not fare as well during a second clash with the Confederate forces at the same house. They were captured by Confederate forces and given a parole after signing an oath not to participate in the war any further. After leaving the Union army around May 2, 1864, Major John C. Eversole and his brother Joseph returned home to Krypton. The rebels either wanted to retaliate for the Yankees' earlier action or were unaware the Eversoles had in fact left the army.

A large group from Caudill's 13th Kentucky Cavalry, a Confederate unit under the command of Major Thomas Chenowith, attacked the Eversole house and killed both Major Eversole and his brother Joseph. Joseph was survived by four children. His wife, Sally Bowling, had died in 1850. Major John C. Eversole was survived by his wife, Nancy Ann Duff, and nine children. Following the second battle, the Eversole poplar log house was riddled with hundreds of bullet holes. Many bullet holes can still be observed in the old house today.

In 1885, French rented Eversole's store building and bought all of his merchandise. The two men signed a contract that Eversole would not compete with French for a period of a year. French claimed that Eversole broke the contract by demanding his store back within ten months. French reluctantly surrendered the building, and secured another location to open a new store.

The typical general merchandise store of that era consisted of a two story building. Many were not even painted. Most had two display windows on each side of the front door. On one side men's clothes were displayed, with women's garments on the other. A canvas awning or a porch roof shaded the front of the building to keep the sunlight from fading the displays. At that time in Hazard, wooden sidewalks bordered each side of the street, which was either dusty or muddy depending on the season. Most general merchandise stores had a small brass bell that tinkled as a person walked through the door. Those entering immediately noticed a blend of smells, including leather, kerosene, coffee, and spices. Long wooden counters stretched along both sides of the building. Drawers and bins built into the counters stored ground sugar, coffee, spices, and seeds. The glass cases on the counter tops displayed more expensive items such as pens, jewelry, perfumes, and silverware. Shelves behind the counters held pots, pans, dishes, bolts of cloth, bottled medicines, and other items. All items were grouped in areas called departments to make things easier for customers to locate.

The nearby county stores sold barreled salt pork (fat back) made from shoulders and sides of lightweight hogs, cut into pieces of about four pounds. This salted fat back, also known as salt bacon, was popular meat before refrigeration.

Additional friction arose between French and Eversole when French became the attorney for land companies outside Perry County that were buying timber through land-lease transactions. Eversole thought the local people were being underpaid for their timber and land. French was an attorney for some non-resident landowners. Joseph Eversole stated that he owned some land claimed by someone French represented. Eversole lost a resulting lawsuit. He blamed French for his defeat and the loss of the land. French accused Eversole of threatening to kill him. Eversole insisted that French tried to hire someone to assassinate him.

A British syndicate was reportedly buying mineral rights to land in Perry County for as little as fifty cents an acre. Timber buyers from outside the region came into southeastern Kentucky purchasing trees from virgin forests at giveaway prices. In addition, mineral rights were selling for next to nothing. So vast were the region's timber supplies and mineral wealth that it took until 1910 to buy up the available resources, all at bargain basement prices.

The land owners had no idea what their timber and minerals were worth. College educated agents bargaining with mostly uneducated mountain residents took advantage of the situation. Sometimes the outside companies hired educated local people to represent them, feeling that a mountain person would likely be more trusted by fellow mountaineers. Most of the buyers of mineral rights were very charming. They spent a lot of time admiring the mountain family's horse and their well-stocked smoke house. They ate with the family and complimented the wife on her wonderful homemade apple butter, saying there was nothing so tasty in the big city. The buyer would spend the night on the family's most comfortable featherbed. By the next morning, the man had no trouble signing away the mineral rights to their property for a very small sum. In most cases the documents would be signed with a duly witnessed "X" by the man. By 1910, non-residents owned a major portion of the land. Absentee investors held as much as three fourths of the remaining timber. The residents of Appalachia sold off eighty-five percent of their mineral rights to outside interests.

At one time, the author's great-grandfather on his mother's side, Alfred Couch, owned a huge part of Browns Fork in Perry County. He was one of the fifteen percent of the large local landowners who did not sell their mineral rights to outside interests. The author inherited a small portion of what had been Alfred Couch's property from his grandmother, Martha Couch, and still retains the mineral rights today. Corporations own most of the mineral rights on the nearby property.

It is obvious why many landowners sold their timber and mineral rights at low prices. Some had received their property free, or for next to nothing. In the late 1800s, court records in Leslie County revealed that several mountaineers purchased fifty acres of land for five cents an acre. Therefore, the prices offered for their stands of timber and their mineral rights seemed high to them.

Every time French and Eversole discussed real estate, mineral rights, and timber prices, they quarreled bitterly. Eversole's loss of land to one of French's clients was particularly galling.

Some three weeks after their Clay City trip, French began an affair that would only escalate the tension. Bill Baker, a clerk in his store, had been keeping company with a young woman. The affair began innocently enough. One afternoon French told his clerk, "Bill, we just got in a shipment of merchandise this afternoon. It's in the back and needs to be stocked on the shelves. Can you stay late tonight and take care of it?"

"But Fult, I promised Gloria I'd take her out to eat tonight. I'm sure she didn't fix herself any supper."

"I'll make sure she gets fed, Bill. If it's all right with you I'll take her to the restaurant across the street. Just a meal, that's all."

"I guess that would be all right, Fult."

Gloria Davis lived alone. Her father had died when she was only five years old and her mother had passed away a year earlier. She was twenty years younger than Fult French. That evening, French drove his buggy up to her house in Hazard's Big Bottom area. He hitched his horse to the white picket fence in front, then went up to her door and knocked.

"Good evening, Miss Davis. I'm Fult French, Bill Baker's boss. Bill had to work late tonight and I've come to take you to dinner if that's all right. Bill was afraid you hadn't fixed a meal for yourself."

"He's right about that, but I can quickly fix something. You don't have to go to that kind of trouble."

Fult French looked at the young woman. She was one of the most beautiful women he had ever seen. Gloria was wearing a nice dress with buttons and bows and a lot of lace. She filled it out like no other woman could. Gloria had the face of an angel, with beautiful black hair hanging shoulder length. "It's no trouble. It will be a pleasure."

"Well, all right. If you insist."

Fult French's wife had never looked like that, even at Gloria's age. They drove downtown in French's buggy.

After the meal, French drove Miss Davis back home. Gloria invited him in and made coffee. As they sat and talked, Gloria decided she really liked this southern man from North Carolina. And, he was wealthy. The woman was in dire financial straits, with the town bank about to foreclose on her house and property.

When Gloria bent forward to pour Fult another cup of coffee, he could see the top of her young, firm breasts as he looked down into the low cut dress. It was more than Fult could take. He grabbed her and kissed her passionately, then threw her onto the couch. When they hit the sofa, Fult sprawled across Gloria's thighs, his hands on the buttons of her dress. The buttons did not obey; Fult's hands felt like he was wearing mittens. Gloria said, "No! I'm not that kind of girl." Fult couldn't hear what she was saying, and after a few moments Gloria didn't seem to be there at all. Five minutes later, the two continued to breathe heavily as they got dressed. Gloria never mentioned a word about her protests to Fult.

That was the beginning of the illicit relationship between Fult French and Gloria Davis. Fult and Gloria always met at the old oak tree at the north end of town where Fult and Joe Eversole had met to go to Clay City. The lovers rode to various locations, such as isolated barns and other secluded spots. Gloria did not want her neighbors seeing French come to her home on a regular basis. Their relationship remained mostly secret, but a few people in town became suspicious. Rumors began to circulate. They made their way to Bill Baker. Gloria had broken off their relationship some time earlier, but Bill continued to wonder what happened. Upon hearing the rumors, he had to be sure. One evening after closing the store, Baker followed French at a distance. As had been done on numerous occasions, French rode straight to the big oak tree where he met Gloria and the two rode off together. That was all Bill Baker needed to see. He decided to make the boss pay for taking his girl away.

"There's somebody at the door, honey," Joe Eversole's wife, Susan, yelled from the kitchen. "Would you get it?"

When Eversole opened the door, there stood Bill Baker. "Hello, Bill, what can I do for you?"

"I'm sorry to bother you at home, Mr. Eversole, but there's something that you ought to know."

"Come on in, Bill."

"Mr. Eversole, I probably shouldn't be here. But I have to warn you. I overheard Mr. French talking to a couple of men in the store. My boss paid them to kill you! French is tired of you trying to interfere with the timber companies he is representing and wants you out of the way. The only way Fult can do that is to make sure you are dead."

"I have trouble believing that, Bill. Fult and I have been friends for a long time. We even went to Clay City together some time ago. I just don't think Fult would do that."

"Mr. Eversole, I swear it! I overheard Mr. French hiring men."

"Bill, if you are so sure that what you say is true, would you prepare an affidavit telling what you just said and sign it?"

"What's an affa-david?"

"That's 'affidavit.' It's a piece of paper simply stating what you heard, with a place left at the bottom to sign. It is something that lawyers use in court. Unless you are willing to legally state that Fult is trying to kill me, I won't believe it."

"Okay, Mr. Eversole, I'll write it out."

Baker prepared the affidavit as Eversole had instructed him. When Eversole read it, he believed that indeed Fult French had hired someone to kill him. The following day, he began recruiting and arming friends and relatives. When French saw what Eversole was doing, he began rounding up his own gunmen.

One person after another joined either the French or the Eversole forces. Some attached themselves out of kinship or friendship, and others as outright mercenaries.

The relationship between Fult French and Gloria Davis ended when the young woman sold her house and moved to Lexington. She became alarmed at the tension between the French and Eversole forces and did not want to be a part of it.

At first, the feud was just a running verbal duel between French and Eversole. However, it was only a few months until one of Fult French's close friends, Silas Gayhart, was killed from ambush while rafting logs on the river. The battle escalated into a full-fledged armed war. Eversole claimed the Gayhart killing was not connected to the feud. He said that no one knew who the killer was. Some people claimed that at least a dozen white men and some Negroes participated in the ambush. Without evidence, no arrests were made and no charges were filed. Although many people in the community claimed they knew the identities of the people involved in the murder, French didn't believe the Eversole family was blameless in the Gayhart slaying. He began to recruit more men. When Eversole saw French adding troops to his army, he followed suit.

Fult French continued to recruit gunmen until his army numbered about seventy. He paid them at the rate of two dollars a day. Reverend Bill Gambrill from Breathitt County, whose family had had trouble with the Eversole family since the Civil War, led the French forces. He preached as hard about killing Eversoles as he did about saving souls. When they were not fighting, French used his mercenaries to cut and harvest timber. During the summer of 1887, several gun battles occurred between the feuding forces, with casualties on both sides. Residents of Perry County quit going to town at night. Many feared going there even in the daylight hours.

The Eversole faction was very surprised to discover one morning that the French faction had left Hazard during the night. Because both French and Eversole were merchants, the feuding hurt their businesses. They were wealthy men only by mountain standards. Both were getting weary of the fighting and the men began entertaining thoughts about a peaceful settlement.

Fult French sent gunslinger Joe Adkins to Joe Eversole's store to see if he would like to talk. Eversole agreed. They met on Big Creek, under a big oak tree similar to the one where the two had met many months before to begin their trip to Clay City.

"How have you been doing, Fult?" Eversole said to French as he got off his horse.

"I'm okay, Joe, but this damn war of ours is costing me too much money."

"It ain't cheap for me either, Fult."

French looked Eversole in the eye as both stood beside their horses, accompanied by armed escorts. "Okay then, what are we going to do about it?"

They continued to talk and eventually drew up a formal truce in which both sides would surrender their firearms. "Joe, if you insist I get rid of my guns, then I will turn them over to the judge over in Leslie County. Does that suit you?"

"Okay, Fult, as long as some of my boys are witnesses."

"You don't trust me, Joe?"

"No, Fult, I don't."

"If I am going to surrender my guns, then who are you going to turn your weapons over to, Joe?"

"Would my father-in-law, Judge Josiah Combs, be all right with you?"

"That would be fine, Joe, but just like you, I want some of my boys to witness the turnover." Their agreement became known as The Treaty of Big Creek.

Both sides turned a large number of weapons over to the two judges in front of witnesses from each camp. However, neither the French nor the Eversole forces believed all the weapons had been surrendered.

The news saying the French-Eversole Feud was over, that the two men had signed a peace treaty, spread quickly throughout Hazard and Perry County. People started returning to town. There was peace, but an uneasy one. The two feuding leaders did turn over some weapons, but they did not release their armies of men, despite the cost of keeping them on. Men working for both French and Eversole could be seen walking the wooden sidewalks of Hazard. Some were still armed.

Many citizens believed the truce would not last long. If a man belonging to the Eversole faction was drinking in a saloon, and a man belonging to the French forces walked in, it got so quiet a person could hear a pin drop!

Several weeks after the peace agreement, French accused Eversole of getting his guns back while Judge Combs was not looking. Eversole said, "French could not get his guns back because of not turning them over in the first place."

The truce was shattered on September 15, 1887. That day, Bill Gambrill, of Breathitt County, came to Hazard and stopped at French's house. Gambrill was known as a gun-slinging part-time preacher who sold moonshine, then preached against "Demon Rum" in his Sunday sermons. As the leader of the French forces, he was willing to fight at a moment's notice. Although from Breathitt County,

Gambrill was well known in Hazard and spent a lot of time there. The story circulated around town that he carried a New Testament in one pocket, a deck of cards in another, a bottle of whiskey in another, and a pistol in yet another pocket. The Eversoles asserted that Gambrill was a worthless character, wanted in Breathitt County on a number of charges. The Eversole family's dislike of Gambrill no doubt stemmed from the troubles the two families had experienced during and after the Civil War.

At the same time, a man named Deane was at French's house along with Gambrill. The sheriff held a warrant against Deane, and went to French's house to arrest him. Gambrill followed the officers to the jail, where he met Joe Eversole. "Joe Eversole, what are you doing in town? I thought the French boys had you scared to show yore face."

Eversole looked Gambrill in the eye. "Listen here you poor excuse for a preacher, if you don't keep your damn mouth shut, I'll shut it for you permanently." One of Eversole's men shot Gambrill from ambush. As Gambrill began to stagger and fall, he drew his pistol. Before Gambrill could fire, Eversole shot him in the head. He died almost instantly, with five bullet holes in his body. John Eversole and Ed Campbell were in a nearby house when the shooting began. Each seized a Winchester and hurried to the scene. Neither took any part in the fight, probably because Gambrill was already dead. The sheriff arrested all three men in the shooting death of Gambrill. Their first trial resulted in a hung jury. They won acquittal in the second.

The feud was on again. By fall, newspapers all over Kentucky—

including Louisville, Lexington, Jackson, and Hazel Green—were reporting that Perry County was again in a state of war, with nearly every family siding with either Eversole or French.

Chapter 5

Tom Takes a Bride

On a cool crisp September day in 1880, leaves were beginning to fall and the colors were spectacular. Some were still green, mixed with orange, red, brown, and yellow. The hills were alive with a rainbow tint.

Tom Smith was twenty years old and would turn twenty-one in a month. He was now a man. Over five feet eight inches tall, with dark brown hair, blue eyes, and a mustache, he was muscular, weighing around 185 pounds. Tom carried himself with dignity by holding his head high as he walked. Today, however, he was not walking. Tom was in Hazard to pick up supplies. He had borrowed a wagon from a Leslie County neighbor who had stipulated that Tom also get supplies for him. Tom and his older sister, Millie, had just moved into the home of their brother, Bill Smith. Bill, who was twenty-three, had married an older woman, named Sarah, from Wooten's Creek, also in Leslie County. Sarah was a widow with a fourteen-year-old daughter named Susan.

Bill and his new family were too poor to own a horse and wagon. Thus Tom enjoyed using the borrowed wagon to go to town. Hazard was only a trading post sort of community, where people came to do business at the courthouse, buy supplies they couldn't raise on their farms, and then go back to their hillside farms to try to scratch out a living from the poor soil. Hazard's population was about 125 people—not much of a town in the eyes of the urban dwellers of the day. Tired of living on the farm, the Perry County seat was paradise to Tom. He volunteered to haul supplies at every opportunity. He simply wanted to go into town.

On this particular day in 1880, he had just loaded his and the neighbor's supplies on the wagon when a young woman came out of Eversole's General Mercantile Store. She was trying to carry a fifty pound bag of flour, and obviously had a problem with its weight. Ordinarily, Tom was not much of a gentleman. He was certainly not the Sir Walter Raleigh type who would take his coat off and lay it across a mud puddle for a lady to walk on. However, as his male hormones were at their peak, and this was one of the most beautiful women ever seen on the streets of Hazard, he climbed off the wagon and ran over to her.

"Miss, I'm Tom Smith. Can I help you?"

The young woman replied, "Thank you, Mr. Smith, I can manage."

"You don't look like you're managing too well to me. Look, I know you don't know me, but I got this here wagon. If you'll let me, I can haul that sack of flour anywhere you want me to. By the way, I didn't catch your name."

"That's because I didn't give it, but if you want to know, I'm Emaline Combs."

"That sure is a purty name, Emaline. I like that."

"I'm glad you do. Okay. This bag is awful heavy. If you want to, put it on the wagon."

With little effort, Tom grabbed the sack of flour and tossed it in the back of the wagon. Then he helped Emaline onto the front seat beside him.

"Where do you live? Where am I taking you and the flour?"

"Oh, my folks live at Lothair. Is that too far for you?"

"No, I'm going to Wooten's Creek over in Leslie County. Did you intend to carry that big bag of flour all the way to Lothair on foot?"

"No, a neighbor was supposed to be in town today, and I was going to get him to haul it, but he didn't show up. To tell you the truth, I didn't know what I was going to do!"

"Well, it's a good thing I showed up, ain't it?" The two talked and talked along the way. Tom was very smitten with her. He drove the horse and wagon to Lothair and stopped at the house Emaline pointed out. It sat on Walnut Point, just above the road. Constructed from rough lumber, it was what was called a "shotgun house," so named because one could open the front and back doors, and then shoot a spray of shotgun pellets the length of the building without hitting anything.

After Tom unloaded the flour bag from the wagon and took it into the house, Emaline introduced him to her parents, George and Maryann Combs, and her seven siblings. One sister, Catherine, was older. Sally and Nancy were younger. All four boys—Elijah, Robert, John, and James—were younger.

Immediately after the introductions, Tom asked Emaline's

parents if he could take her to a barn dance in Leslie County the following Saturday night. They obviously approved of Tom, since they quickly gave permission.

On the remainder of the trip home to Leslie County, Tom floated on air. He couldn't get Emaline Combs out of his mind. Having been out with just a few girls before, he had found them giggly, and not very intelligent. Most of the girls on Wooten's Creek wanted nothing to do with him because of his reputation of being a "crazy" boy who had fits. Emaline didn't know this, of course, and she seemed to really like him.

Tom had met Emaline on a Wednesday, and couldn't wait until Saturday night to borrow the neighbor's wagon to pick her up in Lothair. Planning ahead, Tom tried on his best pair of pants and a shirt to wear to the dance. He asked his sister, Millie, to hold up the one small mirror they had in the house. At a distance, Tom could see himself. He pranced around the house for a good half hour.

Tom's mother, Mary Polly, had died just a few years before. His older sister, Millie, had assumed the duties of family matriarch. She decided to leave Carr's Fork to live with her brother Bill and his new wife on Wooten's Creek after her other siblings—with the exception of Tom—had made new lives for themselves.

She nagged Tom to do his chores, which included cutting the firewood and slopping the hogs. After admiring himself in his good clothes, Tom went outside. He chopped firewood and took it into the kitchen. He grabbed a bucket of slop that Millie had set out, then walked outside to the back of the house, toward the hog pen. He leaned over the wood rail fence to pour the pail of slop in a trough. Tom leaned too far and tumbled into the pen with the hogs. He scrambled out of the hog pen and went into the house. Millie and the others told him to go outside, quickly! They poured several buckets of water over him, trying to get the mud, hog manure, and slop stench off. Tom only had one additional change of clothing. He would have to wear it for the barn dance because the newer clothes could not be cleaned in time. The women of the house did the wash only twice a month. Unfortunately, they had washed everything just a few days before. Millie, Sarah, and Susan refused to immediately wash his clothes, telling him it was stupid to slop the hogs in a good shirt and pants.

Saturday seemed as if it would never come. But when it did, Tom started getting ready early. He took a bath in a wash tub inside the house. The family did not bathe often, especially in the fall and winter. It required heating water and pouring it into a wash tub in the kitchen, always the warmest room in the house because of the big fireplace. In the summer, they used the creek near the house. This was a special occasion, of course, and Tom wanted to smell good, especially after the recent stinky hog pen experience. After the bath, Tom put on his older shirt and pants. He had his sister, Millie, hold up the mirror again so an inspection could be made of himself. Tom's dark brown hair was sticking up in the back. He had heard about the hair tonics they used at the barber shops in Hazard and Hyden, but didn't have anything like that. It suddenly occurred to him what would work. Scooping up some lard from the bucket in the kitchen, Tom ran it through his hair and combed it in as Millie held the mirror. Finally he was satisfied. Tom would have preferred the newer shirt and pants, but this was the best that could be done. He wanted to look his very best for Emaline!

In the small community of Lothair, Emaline was in the back yard of her parents' home above Hazard. She was sitting down on a big rock next to a homemade fireplace. Some rocks had been placed in a half circle. Kindling was set on fire on the ground inside the semi-circle, and then larger chunks of wood were placed on until the fire began to blaze. A tub full of water was placed on the rocks until the water was hot. The water was then poured into another tub with a washboard in it. Each garment was taken out of an old feed sack, placed in the water, rubbed with homemade lye soap, and then scraped on the board until clean. Next, a piece of clothing was pinned on the clothesline to dry. The morning was cool for late September, so the fire felt good. There was a big plum tree near where she was washing the clothes. The leaves had mostly fallen off a week or so ago. One end of the rope clothesline was tied around the plum tree and stretched to an equally leafless barren apple tree on the other end of the yard.

Emaline's mother had given her the laundry as one of her regular tasks. She had done it numerous times, but today the girl wanted to make sure her best dress was especially clean. Late that afternoon, Tom Smith would be picking her up to go to the big dance. She pulled her best dress from the dirty clothes bag. She had forgotten the spilled blackberry cobbler down its front from the Sunday before. After the family got home from church last Sunday, Emaline's mother had told her to pull it off and rinse the stain out. She had not, and now the stain was worse. Emaline thought, I only have one other dress to wear and it is not nearly so nice. Maybe I can sew something over the stain, but I don't have time for that. I have to finish the wash and get ready for the dance. Emaline was truly excited about the dance. This would be her first one as an adult, or nearly an adult. The girl could almost hear her heart pounding and felt funny and light-headed. Emaline could think of nothing but the young man, Tom Smith, who had given her a ride just a few days before and now was taking her to a dance.

The dance would begin at seven o'clock at the Lewis barn on Wooten's Creek. Since it would end late, Tom did not want to take Emaline back to her home that night. He approached Millie. "Sis, is it all right if Emaline Combs, the girl I'm taking to the dance, stays here tonight? It's a long way to Lothair, and I can take her home tomorrow."

"We can make room for her, Tom. Have you asked her about staying the night here?"

"No, but I will ask the parents when I pick her up. They shouldn't mind when I tell them I have a sister, sister-in-law, and step-niece at home."

Tom left his family's home early to go to Lothair, again using the neighbor's horse and wagon. Upon arriving in Lothair, he saw Emaline in front of her house, waiting for him. It had warmed up into a pleasant late afternoon. Emaline was even more beautiful than the first time he saw her, Tom decided. Her face absolutely glowed. Tom asked about spending the night at his family's house. When she asked her parents, they were skeptical at first. After Tom explained that he had a sister, a sister-in-law, and a step-niece at home, they felt more at ease, and said yes. The family admitted they had been concerned about her riding home so late at night.

Tom helped Emaline onto the wagon, and then walked around to get on the other side. He grabbed the reins and gently used them to get the horse moving. After traveling about a mile on the way to Wooten's Creek, Tom said, "Emaline, I wrote a song about you a few days ago. Do you want to hear it?"

"A song about me! I didn't know you wrote songs."

"Well, I'm no professional song writer, but I do like to sit down and write the words of songs that come into my head. Then, I find a tune to sing them with. After meeting you a few days ago, I couldn't get you off my mind, so I sat down and wrote a song."

"Tom, how sweet! Yes! I would like to hear it."

"Now, I ain't got no guitar, fiddle, French harp, or banjur to play the tune. I'll have to sing it like they do in church services around here, with no music."

"That's okay, Tom. I want to hear it."

"Okay, here it is:

When I first saw you
My heart skipped a beat
A beautiful girl
On a Hazard street
You were trying to carry
Too heavy a load
I asked could I help
And you said no

53

Emaline
You are the prettiest girl
I've seen
Your face radiates
Like the morning sun
Emaline
I think you're the one for me

You changed your mind
And I helped with your task
I told you my name
And yours did I ask
And you said

Emaline
You are the prettiest girl
I've seen
Your face radiates
Like the morning sun
Emaline
I think you're the one for me

We rode to your house
And talked about life
And that's when I knew
I wanted you for my wife

Emaline
You are the prettiest girl
I've seen
Your face radiates
Like the morning sun
Emaline
I think you're the one for me
Yes, Emaline
I know you're the one for me."

"Tom, that's a wonderful song," Emaline said. She moved closer on the wagon seat. Tom put his arm around her, and then briefly kissed her lips.

Emaline looked Tom straight in the eyes and told him, "I'm not sure about that wife part in your song. Don't you think it's a little fast? After all, this is only the second time we've met."

"When I write songs I try to say what I am feeling deep inside. That is what I felt when I wrote it. Emaline, there was just something special the first time I laid eyes on you."

"I just think we ought to go out a few times before we talk about getting married."

"Okay, Emaline."

"Tom, my family and close friends just call me Emma. Could you please just call me Emma?"

"I sure will Emma. I'm glad you consider me a close friend."

As they rode along the rutted-out road toward Wooten's Creek, the couple talked non-stop. When they reached their destination, Tom helped Emma—as she was to him now—off the wagon and introduced her to the people who had arrived at the Lewis barn early. It was now six o'clock, a full hour before the festivities would get underway. The early arrivals stared at the girl that Tom had brought. After all, most unattached young women in the community would have nothing to do with Tom Smith. In other words, "They were as scarce as hen's teeth." Not only that, but this young lass was beautiful.

When the dance started, Tom and Emma spent most of the time talking on the sidelines like two wallflowers. Tom, not the most socially acceptable young man in the community, had been to very few barn dances. He knew little about square dancing. Emma didn't know much more, but the two were never at a loss for words for each other. The running sets were too fast, but they did get onto the floor a couple of times for the Virginia reel. Also, Emma and Tom frequently went to the refreshment table. Absorbed in each other, they didn't notice that most of the people were staring holes through them.

The square dance caller asked for the crowd's attention. "I've got a special announcement for you folks. There will be a pie supper right here in the Lewis barn a week from tonight. It will start at six in the evening. You all come!"

Tom didn't waste time. "Emma, would you like to come to the pie supper next Saturday?"

"Tom, I'd love to."

As the couple left the dance that night, the crowd was still staring at them. They were already so in love that they neither noticed nor cared about the stares. On the trip earlier from Emma's house to the Lewis barn, Tom had briefly touched her lips with a kiss. However, on the trip from the barn to his house where Emma would spend the night, Tom kissed her again. This time the two embraced and shared a deep and passionate kiss. When their lips parted, Emma looked at Tom. "That was wonderful, Tom, but we should stop. You mentioned marriage in your song. Are you serious? Do you really want to marry me?"

"Emma, I've never asked a girl to marry me before, but yes, I'm dead serious. I want you to be my wife!"

"Let me think about it, Tom."

"Take all the time you need."

It was dark, but there was a full moon when Tom pulled the wagon up to the barn near his family's home. He tied up the horse, and then walked Emma by the moonlight to the front door of the house where he introduced her to his sister Millie, sister-in-law Sarah, step-niece Susan, and his brother Bill. Tom then went out to put the horse in the barn. The neighbor had agreed to let him keep the horse and wagon for the night so he could take Emma back to Lothair the next day.

Susan told Emma that she and Millie shared a bed. Emma could sleep with her in the bed and Millie would make a pallet on the floor out of her mother's old featherbed. Emma immediately liked Millie and Susan. She had not talked to Tom's brother that much, but he seemed nice.

After Tom unhitched the horse from the wagon and put it in the barn, he came back to the house and went to bed. The day had been a long one. All he said to Bill was "goodnight" before falling asleep.

The next morning Millie and Sarah fixed a big breakfast of ham and eggs. They usually didn't have meat for breakfast, but Sarah decided to get some of the cured ham out of the smokehouse because Emma was eating with them. Tom didn't mention that he had asked Emma to marry him. The conversation around the table consisted of small talk. After breakfast, Emma offered to help wash the dishes. Millie declined her offer. "Sarah and I can do the dishes. Tom had better get you back home before your folks start worrying. Anyhow, he has to get the horse and wagon back to Mr. Lewis."

On their way to Emma's home at Lothair, Tom asked, "Is it all right if I pick you up for the pie supper at about the same time next Saturday?"

"Yes, Tom. That would work out fine. I don't think my parents will care if I spend the night again at your house. I really liked your family."

"That's good because I hope they will be your family. When are you going to let me know about us getting married?"

"I'll let you know, one way or the other, when you pick me up next Saturday."

When Tom dropped Emma off at her house, she asked her parents about going to the pie supper the next Saturday and again staying the night at his family's house. They readily agreed. Tom was ecstatic! On the way back to Wooten's Creek, he kept singing the song he had written for Emaline. She had not yet said yes to his proposal, but he knew deep down that she would.

The next week seemed to fly by for Tom. All he had on his mind was Emma. Finally, it was Saturday. Tom went to a nearby store to get some flour and salt for Millie. When he returned, Millie met him just inside the front door, holding up the good shirt and pants he had worn when he fell into the hog pen.

"Me and Sarah wanted to surprise you. We decided to wash the good clothes you messed up when you fell into the hog pen. You can wear them tonight when you take Emma to the pie supper. We like her and Bill says he does too. Are you going to ask her to marry you?"

"I already have, Millie."

"Well, she didn't say no or you wouldn't be taking her to the pie supper tonight."

"She didn't say yes either. She's supposed to let me know when I pick her up this afternoon."

"I sure hope she says yes," Millie said.

"I do too, Millie. I've never met anybody like her." Tom grabbed his sister and hugged her. "Thanks for washing my clothes. Thank Sarah for me, too."

After donning his freshly washed clothes, Tom left for Lothair at about the same time as the week before. Again, Emma was waiting outside the house. Upon arrival he noticed Emma still had that angelic smile and was wearing a different dress, a nicer one, than she had worn the week before. She held a large box in both hands. "What's that for?"

"Well, Tom Smith, where do you think we are going anyway?"

"A pie supper. Oh, that's a pie!"

"I hope you are the winning bidder, Tom. I don't want to eat it with anyone but you."

"I know what the box looks like. I don't have much money, but I'll spend what I have to bid on it."

Tom helped Emma onto the wagon seat beside him. That same seat she had taken the day he had first met her in Hazard with the big bag of flour. Emma said nothing. After about a mile, Tom said, "The suspense is killing me. Have you decided whether or not you will marry me?" Tom looked at Emma with a forlorn look on his face. "Well?"

"Yes, Tom. Yes, I will marry you!"

Tom grabbed Emma, embraced her and kissed her. When they

came up for breath, Tom was beaming and grinning from ear to ear!

When they got to the Lewis barn, Tom tied up the horse and wagon, then helped Emma down. Tom and Emma paid attention only to each other as they talked about their imminent new life together. They didn't notice a young man paying close attention to the decorated pie box that Emma was carrying.

The pie supper got started right on time. Three boxes were auctioned off, then Emma's was placed on the table. Tom immediately bid two cents. A young man in the back shadows shouted, "Three cents." The bids went back and forth until it got up to thirty-five cents, Tom's final bid. That was all his money.

The persistent bidder in the back apparently did not know that Tom was tapped out. He upped the ante sharply, bidding fifty cents. Tom could not top this bid, so the box, the pie, and its cook's company for dinner went to the bidder in the back of the barn. Tom was upset that someone else was going to get to eat the pie with Emma. All through the bidding, Tom had wondered who this man was and why he was willing to pay that much for the pie. None of the earlier pies had gone for more than twenty-five cents. When the high bidder came forward, Tom fully understood his interest in Emma's pie. He was Cletus Couch, one of the two boys Tom had whipped years earlier when they attacked him on his way to the store. Cletus had not forgotten that whipping. Tom decided, I won't forget this either.

After the pie supper, as Tom helped Emma onto the wagon seat, she said, "I'm sorry I had to eat my pie with that nasty looking young man."

"It wasn't your fault that I didn't have enough money to outbid him, Emma. You know the Couch boy did that for meanness, don't you?"

"For meanness? What are you talking about, Tom?"

"Cletus used to live at Carr's Fork; he just recently moved here. Well, back a few years ago, Cletus and a buddy of his waylaid me as I was walking to the store. They wanted to beat me up. I whipped both of them. I guess Cletus hasn't forgotten it. Well, Emma, I won't forget what he done tonight, you can bet your bottom dollar on that."

"Tom, forget about it. It was just a pie, and besides, we can eat pies together for the rest of our lives. Do you have a particular date in mind for our wedding?"

"No, but I do want to wait until after Christmas. What about sometime in January?"

"It's awful cold in January; maybe in February, toward the end of the month when it starts warming up a little bit," Emma said as she looked into Tom's face.

"Emma, it doesn't really matter, whenever you want."

"Okay, let's make it February twenty-fourth. I would like to have a new dress to get married in and that will give mother plenty of time to make me one. We'll get married at the courthouse in Hazard."

The two talked until approaching the Smith house. They announced their wedding plans upon entering the door. Millie and Sarah squealed and hugged them both. When Emma told them she wanted her mother to make a new dress, Millie and Sarah began making suggestions as to the style. Susan also offered an opinion.

Emma told the Smith family that she had not announced the marriage decision to her parents, but was sure of their approval because they seemed to like Tom.

Emma was right! Both parents were pleased she was marrying Tom, and her mother insisted on making the wedding dress.

On February 24, 1881, Tom picked up Emma in the same borrowed wagon. This time it was their wedding day. He wore a recently acquired suit with a string tie. The bride looked beautiful in the simple white wedding dress her mother had made. About halfway to Hazard, Emma said, "Tom, some friends of ours stopped by this morning and told us about a fire at the Couch place. It that where the Cletus Couch who bought my pie lived?"

"Yes. His family just recently moved to Wooten's Creek from Carr's Fork. He was still living at home. I heard about the fire. It happened two days ago. It's too bad. I don't think they got much stuff out. Lucky nobody was hurt."

The wedding took place at the Perry County Courthouse. One of the people who would become Tom's bitter enemy, Perry County Circuit Court Clerk Ira J. Davidson, signed the marriage certificate as one of the witnesses.

The Smiths and their neighbors on Wooten's Creek gave the young couple a shivaree. A typical mountain shivaree takes place in the evening after the ceremony, when the married couple goes home. As soon as the lights are blown out, the neighbors go crazy. Surrounding the house, the participants create as great a commotion as possible, banging on pots and pans, playing any musical instruments they can get their hands on, and of course, yelling and screaming far into the night. There are records of people bringing shotguns and dynamite to a shivaree, for maximum disturbance value.

Chapter 6

Tom Joins the French Cause

Tom and Emma moved to the Bill and Sarah Smith homestead with Tom's sister Millie, and step-niece Susan. Ten months after their wedding day, Emma gave birth to a baby girl they named Matilda.

Tom still occasionally had seizures. His brother, Bill, taught Emma how to deal with Tom when he was having a "fit" to keep him from injuring himself.

When Matilda was three years old, Tom finally convinced Emma they should move to Hazard. He had always liked town life. Tom still went to Hazard every chance he got. Emma preferred country living. When she reluctantly agreed to move, Tom said he would go into Hazard to find a place for them to live. It was a growing community. Everybody said it was just a matter of time until the railroad came. Then, Hazard would be a boomtown!

Tom started asking questions about houses that might be for rent. He discovered an old house just to the south of town that the owner was willing to rent to a family. Emma loved the place. It needed a lot of cleaning, but she saw potential. Emma lacked neither energy nor initiative. As a girl, she had been given many chores; hard work came naturally. She began putting in long hours on the house. Even the landlord was impressed, and pleased that he had rented the place to such an industrious young couple. Tom did some of the work on the place, but only when Emma nagged him.

A year after the Smiths moved to Hazard, Emma gave birth to another child, a boy they called Bud. A year later another daughter—Maggie—arrived, followed by son John. Three years later, Cody was born. Edgar, the sixth child, arrived three years after Cody.

Claiming to be looking for work, Tom spent a lot of time rambling around Hazard. He found some odd jobs, but they didn't pay much. However, he somehow earned enough to buy food for the family and to pay the rent.

On election day in the spring of 1884, Tom noticed a small crowd gathered around a speaker. He moved through the crowd until he could see a man standing close to a soap box, next to Blue Bill Black, a candidate for Jailer. Tom had heard of Blue Bill, but didn't know him. He had seen him walking up and down the road shouting, "Snake oil, snake oil, buy one and I'll give you two free." Old Blue Bill made his living by peddling, selling anything and everything. Tom stopped to hear what the candidate had to say.

A man of about six feet eight inches tall was doing Blue Bill's introduction. Tom thought to himself, I bet that feller has to stoop down when he goes through a door. After the introduction, Blue Bill got on the soap box. "Yes sir, tank all you ladies and gentlemens. I'm still on the ballot fer Jailer on Democrat ticket. I was born on Polecat in a dirt floor, and evertime I cross over someone's door sill, they say, 'There's Blue!' And this is Blue. I'll make you a goodun. I pulled over fifty months in these here jails, and it's me. Still say it's Blue, a blue-bloodied man. Don't forget me now; make em Jailer, a true un!"

Tom knew Blue Bill would get only a handful of votes. Obviously someone had talked him into running in order to take a few votes away from the opponent of the candidate they really wanted to win, as well as to have some fun. Tom knew what it was like to be ridiculed. A large segment of the population of Carr's Fork had made fun of him, much as the people in Hazard were making fun of ole Blue Bill. Tom empathized with the old peddler.

Tom and Emma and little Matilda (who they called "Tildy") had been living in Hazard for several months. He walked into Hazard often and had made a number of friends among the shady element in the community. After Blue Bill finished his campaign speech and the crowd was dispersing, some shots rang out.

"What the hell's going on?" Tom said aloud, but to no one. He saw that several of his friends were being shot at from outside the polling place. Tom slithered behind the nearest man firing at his friends. He picked up a sizable rock and hit the man over the head, knocking him unconscious.

"You won't be shooting at nobody for a while, you bastard," he told the unconscious man. Tom picked up the man's gun and shot the other two men from behind, which put a sudden end to the gunfight.

He left three wounded men in the streets of Hazard that day. The news quickly spread through town. Tom's fame radiated like wildfire. People in Hazard began to openly refer to him as Bad Tom Smith.

Tom, Emma, and Matilda remained in Hazard. He continued to

work some odd jobs, barely making enough money to take care of his family. Tom got involved in some small scrapes with some of the town toughs, reinforcing his newfound reputation as a "bad" man.

When the French-Eversole Feud started, both sides began to recruit men. Bad Tom Smith's name appeared at the top of both the Eversole and French lists. Joe Eversole personally looked up Bad Tom to offer him a job with his gang. He waited for Tom to leave his house and introduced himself.

"Mr. Smith, I'm Joe Eversole. Perhaps you have heard of me?"

"Yeah, Mr. Eversole, I think everybody in Hazard has heard of you and Fult French, what with this feud you all got going on."

"That's what I wanted to talk to you about Tom. Is it all right if I call you Tom?"

"It's okay with me. After all, that's what my parents called me."

"Tom, I heard what you did to those three men earlier this year. People tell me you are the best shot in this part of the state. I would like you to join our forces. I can pay you well. You're the type of man that we need to make sure the French gang don't wipe us out."

"Well, I appreciate your offer, Mr. Eversole, but I really don't want to get involved in the war between you and Mr. French. It don't have nothing to do with me, and I just as soon stay out."

"Okay, Tom, but if you change your mind, let me know."

"I will, Mr. Eversole."

Fult French sent one of his hired hands to offer Bad Tom a position. Smith turned French down too. He didn't want to fight in a feud that didn't personally involve himself.

In 1887, Tom decided he needed a horse. His family had been living in the house south of town for about two years and he had not been able to find steady work. Tom had been through three jobs, but always found a reason to quit. Worse, he still had to walk everywhere.

Tom began eying the businesses in Hazard for a good-looking horse to easily steal. One day, he noticed a horse tied up behind Joe Eversole's store. Tom learned that it belonged to Joe Eversole's brother-in-law. A few days later, after dark, when the brother-in-law was working late, Tom helped himself to the horse and rode off. One of Joe Eversole's cousins saw Bad Tom Smith ride down Main Street on the horse. He contacted A.G. Duff, the Hazard Town Marshall. Duff went to the Smith house. When he knocked on the door, Emma answered.

"Mrs. Smith, I'm sorry to bother you but I need to talk to your husband."

"Tom just came in a few minutes ago. He should be back in our bedroom."

"Is it all right if I go back?"

"Sure, it's right through there." Emma pointed toward the back of the house.

Duff walked through the house with his hand on his gun. He had heard of what Bad Tom Smith had done to those three men in Hazard. Duff didn't want to end up like them. He knocked on the door, gun in hand.

"Tom Smith, this is Marshall Duff, I want to talk to you."

"Come on in Marshall," Tom shouted.

Duff entered.

"There's no need for a weapon, Marshall. What's on your mind?"

"Do you own a horse?" Duff asked Smith.

"Yes. I just bought one today. It's tied up in the back."

"Let's go see it," Duff told Smith. The two men walked behind the building, where the horse was tied.

"That looks like a horse that belongs to Joe Eversole's brother-in-law, Nicholas Combs. You got any papers for it?" Duff asked Smith.

"No, I didn't know you needed any papers. I bought it from a man who said he was passing through town.

"Well, if you don't have any papers, I'm going to take you to jail because I think you stole it. As far as I'm concerned, there's nothing worse than a horse thief!" Duff got on his horse. Tom was forced to walk, at gunpoint, up Main Street to the jail, where he was put in a cell. Duff then walked over to Eversole's store and told Combs, the owner of the horse, that he had recovered the animal, and it appeared that Bad Tom Smith had stolen it.

The next day Combs filed papers to prosecute Smith for stealing his horse. When word of Bad Tom Smith's arrest for stealing an Eversole family member's horse spread to Fult French, he didn't waste any time contacting the Perry County Judge. After talking to the judge for a few minutes, French was able to secure a full pardon for Smith.

The case was thrown out of court and Bad Tom Smith was released from jail. Joe Eversole had a lot of influence in Hazard and Perry County, but Fult French had even more influence and did not hesitate to use it. The Eversole family was angry that Bad Tom Smith got away with stealing a horse, but there was nothing legally they could do about it.

Bad Tom got outraged because the Eversole family had decided to prosecute him as a horse thief. He was grateful to Fult French for pulling strings to get him out of the mess. Smith, who had just a few months before turned down both men's efforts to recruit him, made a trip to Fult French's store immediately upon being released from jail. He walked in and asked the clerk, "Is Mr. French in?"

"Yes, he's in the back. Would you like for me to get him?"

"Yes, tell him Tom Smith is here to see him."

A few moments later Fult French walked into the front of the store. "Tom, Tom Smith, it's good to see you. What can I do for you?"

"It's not what you can do for me, Mr. French. It's what I can do for you. You asked me to join your forces a few months ago, and I said no. I've changed my mind and my services are yours if you still want me."

"I do still want you, Tom. Welcome aboard."

Bad Tom's fearless demeanor and superior sharp shooting skills made him the most dangerous man in the French army. However, some of the other gang members didn't know that at first. Tom thought he still needed to prove himself.

Shortly after joining the group, Tom spotted a member of the Eversole gang, James Davidson. He noticed that Davidson kept looking at his pocket watch. Tom liked the watch's looks. It was high time for him to get one. One day, Tom followed Davidson into an alley and pulled a pistol. He relieved Davidson of the watch, then dared him to do anything about it. Davidson reported the robbery to the authorities, but again French pulled the right strings. Tom decided to teach Davidson a lesson for having reported the theft.

Tom went to the French house one night and told Fult, "I think you're going to like this. Guess whose house went up in flames tonight?"

French said, "I don't know, Tom, you tell me."

Bad Tom said, "That son of a bitch Davidson's mother's house. That's who. That will learn him to mess with me!" Bad Tom didn't stop at telling French about torching the house. He bragged about it all over Hazard. Soon all of Hazard regarded Bad Tom Smith as the leader of the Fult French gang.

Chapter 7

A Reign of Terror in Hazard

Tom Smith was not the only "bad" man in Hazard and Perry County. Joe Hurt had built a reputation rivaling Bad Tom's. He had pulled a few robberies and wounded a couple of men. The local population feared him. Hurt enjoyed his newfound fame. He decided it would be good business to team up with Bad Tom. In 1887, Hurt went to Bad Tom's house while Emaline and the children were visiting a neighbor. He made Tom a proposition.

"Tom, what we need to do is make some real money instead of this nickel and dime stuff we've been doing alone. I've got an idea how both of us can get rich overnight and not have to worry about this stupid feud between French and Eversole."

"What do you mean stupid feud? Fult French shore hain't stupid!"

"I know that Tom, but is he yore kin?"

"No, Fult ain't kin to me, but he has been a good friend. I'm loyal to my friends."

"Okay, if you want to be loyal to Fult, I don't care. But what I've got in mind can make us both a lot of money."

"What have you got in mind, Joe?"

"The L&E train coming into Winchester next week will be

carrying a lot of money. It's a shipment of new bills for the banks in Jackson and Hazard. Now, it would be hard to hold up the train because they got them damn railroad detectives. But the shipment to the Jackson and Hazard banks will have to be brought by wagon. There are plenty of places to attack the wagon and take the money."

"There's only one thing wrong with yore plan, Joe."

"What's that?"

"Fult French owns part of the Hazard bank. I ain't about to be stealing his money. He's been too good to me."

"What the hell do you care about Fult French? If you don't want to pull the job, I'll round up some other boys to help me. I'm getting that money."

"That's what you think." Tom quickly pulled a gun from his holster in a smooth, rhythmic motion and fired two shots into Hurt's chest. Hurt fell over dead.

Bad Tom had built a reputation on the three men wounded when he first came to Hazard. The trail of crime and vice that his Fult French gang left behind in Perry County was well known. However, Joe Hurt was the first man Tom actually killed. When the people in Hazard learned of the murder of Joe Hurt at Tom Smith's house, they breathed a sigh of relief. The citizens were glad that at least one of the two bad men was dead.

The county sheriff and the prosecutor brought no charges against Smith. That was because of the overwhelming influence of Fult French in Hazard and Perry County, and the opinion of most people that Bad Tom had rendered the community a service by killing

Hurt. The murder of Hurt expanded the stature of Tom Smith's bad reputation.

Joe Eversole had at one time been Fult French's closest friend, but now he was French's most bitter enemy. French decided it was time for Eversole to die. French now had the services of Bad Tom Smith and Smith was just the man for the job!

Fult rode to Tom Smith's house just outside of Hazard, dismounted, and knocked on the door.

"Tom, are you home?"

"Is that you, Fult? Well, come on in."

"I can only stay for a minute, Tom. There's something I want you to do for me."

"All you have to do is name it."

"I been thinking. That son of a bitch Joe Eversole has got to go. I want him dead. I want you to kill him for me, Tom."

"Okay, I'll do it for you. But it's gonna be hard to catch him alone. He's got a lot of protection."

"I don't want you to do it alone. Take three of my boys. You pick 'em. Get three of my best. I want you men to track that Eversole bastard, but don't let him know it. When he lets his guard down, kill him. It might take you several days, but I want it done."

"I'll do it, Fult. You can count on me."

Bad Tom picked three of French's men. They found Eversole's trail and followed him for several days. Eversole knew his life was in danger. He had known it since the feud began and had surrounded himself with bodyguards. However, he did not know that Bad Tom and three others were now closing in on him for the kill.

One bright summer morning the birds were active and Joe Eversole thought it was a great day to be alive. The trees were beautiful and there was not a cloud in the light blue sky. The mountain air was sweet to breathe and the birds were singing in the trees.

Every day since the feud began, Eversole had been riding to his store in Hazard surrounded by enough armed men so that no one would be foolish enough to start anything.

Eversole was weary of having so many bodyguards around. On this morning, wanting to enjoy the day, Joe asked his best marksman, Nicholas Combs, to ride with him into Hyden, located in Leslie County.

"Joe, don't you want the other men to ride with you this morning?" Eversole's wife, Susan, asked when she found out that only one bodyguard was going.

"No, honey. I don't think there's much danger. Old Fult knows better than to go after me personal."

"I think you ought to take the other bodyguards."

"It'll be all right, honey, you'll see."

Tears streamed down Eversole's wife's cheeks as Joe Eversole, Judge Josiah Combs, and the judge's nephew, Nicholas Combs, rode off. Eversole and the judge planned to attend the circuit court session at Hyden, in Leslie County, where they had been members of the bar for several years. As the group rode up Big Creek, Judge Combs, Eversole, and Nicholas Combs were joined by Officer Tom Hollifeld, who was taking a female prisoner, Mary Jones, to Hyden. Judge

Combs, Hollifeld, and Jones rode on ahead, passing by Dark Hollow, the best place for an ambush.

Bad Tom and the three other French gang members were squatting in some tall bushes. They spotted Eversole and Nicholas Combs approaching.

"Boys, that's old Joe Eversole, and the bastard has only got one man with him. This is what we've been waiting for," whispered Bad Tom.

Joe Eversole was still admiring the beauty of the day—listening to the birds sing and breathing in the fresh mountain air—when the stillness of the day was shattered by gunfire from a hillside above. The birds quit singing as bullets from three Winchesters and a shotgun sunk into the flesh of Eversole and Combs. Both fell from their saddles into the mud. Combs fell over his horse's head, seriously bleeding from three wounds. Bad Tom Smith ran quickly to Eversole and searched his dead body. He emptied the pockets of the corpse, taking everything of any value. The Eversole family claimed that between 250 and 300 dollars was taken from Joe Eversole's body. Smith, during his confession at his hanging, said he took only thirty dollars from Eversole.

Smith then began to search the pockets of Combs. During the search, Combs, who was not dead but very weak, regained consciousness and looked up at Smith.

"Tom, Tom Smith. Why did you shoot me? I ain't done nothing to you. I thought you was my friend. Tom, Tom, don't shoot me anymore for I am dying fast enough."

Smith looked Combs straight in the face. "Nick, it's too bad you were with old man Eversole, because now you ain't gonna be nobody's friend anymore 'cause I can't leave no witnesses." Bad Tom pulled his pistol and shot Combs in the head. The bullet went through Combs's right temple and out his left. It passed so close to the eyes that it cut the muscles holding them in place. Both eyeballs rolled out.

When shot, Nick Combs was riding his mother's big bay horse, John. Bad Tom had earlier stolen Nick's horse and escaped trial for the theft. The riderless bay took off for its owner's house, a distance of about five miles. It crossed Big Creek, went through Browns Fork, crossed Town Mountain, forded the North Fork of the Kentucky River, then went through a section of Hazard to get home.

When Alice Combs, Nick's mother, noticed that the animal had blood on its saddle, she took her apron off and threw it on the saddle. The woman rode to Big Creek and found her son laying in the road, near death. Nick lived for a few minutes after she located him. Malta Ellen Davidson, a niece of Nick Combs, remembers as a child seeing her aunt, Alice, stuffing cotton into the eye sockets of her son before his funeral. A posse was formed by the county sheriff, but Bad Tom and the other men had a long head start and escaped. An examination of the ambush site revealed that the assassins had been camping there for a few days, because remains of meals were discovered at the location. The murders occurred about a mile from the mouth of Browns Fork, near the site of the present day Big Creek Baptist Church.

Earlier, Eversole's wife, Susan, had taken her three young

children to church. The two oldest sons, Cassius and John B., were in Virginia studying at law school. Her husband was a merchant, and always insisted that she wear nice clothes. When Joe died, Susan had on a nice taffeta dress. At that time, the church's minister was a visiting preacher. Mrs. Eversole was to serve dinner (lunch) to the minister, and had a fine meal already set on the table. When a man arrived, he told those at the house that Joe Eversole had been killed. After hearing the news, Mrs. Eversole took her children and left them at church to later be picked up. They could spend the day with her aunt, Sarah Hundly, who was keeping house for her dead sister's husband.

Huge crowds attended the funerals of Joe Eversole and Nicholas Combs. The Eversole faction stationed numerous guards at Joe's funeral in case of trouble. Both ceremonies proceeded without incident.

Bad Tom recalled the details of the shooting of Eversole and Combs to a woman he thought he could trust. She did not keep his secret. Smith would later admit that the killing of Combs bothered him more than any of the other murders he had been involved in. The other three members of the French gang shook their heads at what they had seen. They could not believe Bad Tom would murder, in cold blood, a man he had called his friend. The three were very careful not to talk about what they witnessed, fearing that Bad Tom would come after them. But the story got around anyhow.

When the news reached the Eversole clan, they decided that it was time to take care of Bad Tom Smith. Ira Davidson, Joe Eversole's son-in-law, was still upset about Bad Tom's theft of a horse, and worse, his getting away with it. And now Smith had killed his father-in-law and another man. Davidson would do all he could to bring him to justice.

Davidson sent word to the three men who had been with Bad Tom at the ambush. When they came to the Eversole stronghold, Davidson said, "Boys, I hear you been telling how Bad Tom Smith shot Nicholas Combs in cold blood following that ambush the other day. I could kill you bastards right now for taking part in that ambush that left my father-in-law dead, but I don't want you. I want Bad Tom Smith and Fult French."

One of the men spoke up. "Mr. Davidson, we was just obeying Mr. French's orders in that ambush. But we just can't go along with shootin' down a man like Bad Tom did."

Davidson said, "Here's what I got to offer you boys. If you testify against Bad Tom Smith, I will pay each of you a hundred dollars. And I'll make sure you're not prosecuted for the murders of Joe Eversole and Nicholas Combs. A hundred dollars is a lot of money, boys."

The three agreed to take the money with the understanding that they would not be charged with murder. Davidson used the Eversole family's influence to have Bad Tom Smith charged with two counts of murder. The Perry County Sheriff brought Smith before a magistrate who filed the charges, but released him on bond. While out on bail, Bad Tom found the three French men who had agreed to testify against him.

"Boys, I thought you was my friends. I don't know what them

Eversole bastards promised you for talkin' against me in court. I can promise this: if you testify against me, you will be three dead sons of bitches."

The three went to the courthouse to find the Perry County Prosecutor. They said they had been mistaken about what they had seen. Therefore, they could not be witnesses in Tom Smith's trial. The prosecutor had no choice. He dropped the charges.

The dismissal of murder charges emboldened Bad Tom. The outlaw now believed he could do anything with impunity. Smith decided to even an old score with Shade Combs. Bad Tom trailed Combs for several days. When Combs became aware Smith was stalking him, his blood ran cold. Combs began holing up inside his log cabin. After several days of staying inside, he decided Bad Tom must have given up the pursuit. So Combs went outside to play with his children. Even if Bad Tom was waiting in the woods, he thought, Smith wouldn't shoot with children around. Combs was standing beside his little daughter when he slumped to the ground after being hit by a gunshot. He had underestimated Bad Tom Smith's doggedness and his capacity for evil. The Combs children ran inside. Bad Tom and other members of the Fult French gang came into Shade Combs's yard to make sure he was dead.

The county sheriff arrested Tom Smith for the murder of Shade Combs. The court released him without charges. Fult French now obviously and completely controlled Hazard and Perry County.

The French forces were not alone in the tactical use of ambushes. On October 9, 1888, Elijah Morgan, a member of the French forces, was shot and killed from ambush just two miles from Hazard. Many people in the area regarded Morgan as a man of courage and determination. On the morning of Morgan's death, he and Frank Grace had been riding to Hazard to try to conclude a tentative agreement with members of the Eversole forces.

Following Joe Eversole's death, his brothers—Judge George W. and John C.—took over leadership of the Eversole faction. John C. Eversole taught school for a while, and also worked as a drummer, selling various goods for a Cincinnati company. John Campbell helped the Eversoles by keeping the hired guns in line.

Fult French wanted to settle some scores. Bad Tom owed French for keeping him out of jail. French sent for him. "Tom, it's good to see you again. I've got another job for you to do."

"What is it, Fult?"

"Well, I thought when we got rid of Joe Eversole, things would settle down. The two Eversole brothers took over, but they didn't know how to do anything without John Campbell. John was a good organizer. Not too long ago, those idiots Eversole hired accidentally shot Campbell to death. Campbell had set up a password, and one night he forgot it. They shot him to death. Now, Ambrose Amburgy has got the Eversoles all steamed up again, and they are starting to be a problem. I want you to kill Amburgy."

"Okay, if that's what you want, Fult. That Amburgy has been an Eversole man for years. I'll make sure he won't bother you anymore."

"Good, Tom. I can always count on you!"

Bad Tom decided not to use any of Fult French's gang this time.

He talked his brother Bill into riding to Hindman with him. He had heard that Ambrose Amburgy would be there on business.

Tom and Bill went to a house on Main Street in Hindman, hid in the cellar, and waited. They knew Amburgy would be going to the courthouse. He would have to pass by a small window in that house's cellar to get there. They waited in the cellar for two hours before spotting Amburgy on the street. When he passed, Bad Tom and Bill fired three shots, one hitting Amburgy in the neck. Although badly wounded, Amburgy would recover.

Bad Tom was arrested for the shooting. Because it took place in Knott County, the Eversole family thought they might have better luck getting Smith tried for attempted murder. However, the Fult French influence was as strong in Hindman and Knott County as it was in Hazard and Perry County. No charges were brought against Bad Tom.

The French forces controlled Hazard, and the Perry County Sheriff could not keep order because of what many people claimed were these "low down, mighty sorry kind of men." The courts were paralyzed, even at the State level. In Frankfort, Kentucky's capital, Governor Simon Buckner heard that the situation in Perry County was so bad that the circuit judge had shut down his court. He summoned the head of the State Militia, Colonel James King, to his office.

"Come on in, Jim, have a seat."

"Thank you, Governor."

"Jim, I've got a job for you to do. You've probably heard about the little war going on up in Perry County."

"Yes, Governor. What about it?"

"Jim, normally I'm content to let the hillbillies up there kill themselves off, but the situation is out of hand. I understand that this fellow, Fult French, has complete control over the town and the county. The only law there now is what he says. All the elected officials have either been killed or forced to leave town. The law abiding citizens are in a panic. There is a lot of coal in that region. Someday the railroads will haul it out, which will immensely improve the economy of this state. But that can't happen in the absence of law and order. The circuit judge up there, H.C. Lilly, has asked me to send in the militia. He can't even conduct trials. People are afraid to testify. Judge Lilly says he needs troops to keep the peace and open the courts. I telegraphed him. I said that a small group of feuding mountaineers shouldn't keep the sheriff and the judge from discharging their duties. However, the latest reports indicate the situation is even worse than what the judge said it was. As quickly as you can, send a thousand troops to Hazard. Get them there quickly, so order can be restored. Arrest those who committed crimes during this war and bring them to trial."

Colonel King said, "That's a tall order, Governor, but I'll start on it right away."

Colonel King left Governor Buckner's office and called on General Sam Hill to pass on the governor's instructions.

General Hill hurriedly assembled the troops and placed Captain James Sohan in charge.

Two weeks after Governor Buckner's meeting with Colonel King, the first troops arrived in Hazard. The troops had difficulty getting there. They first boarded two passenger cars and used one baggage car on the L&N Railroad in Louisville. Six hours later, at about two in the morning, the troops arrived at London, Kentucky. The passenger cars were sidetracked and the troops stayed in them until daylight. After breakfast, the soldiers started on the seventy-five-mile trip from London to Hazard. They traveled in fourteen wagons with teams. One team pulled a Gatling gun. The officers rode horses. In some places, the road was almost impassable! The troops frequently had to help the teams up the hills and over rough or excessively soft places. On the second day, Judge Lilly joined the procession. It took five days to reach Hazard. The soldiers found the Perry County Courthouse grounds unsuitable, so they set up camp about 200 yards away, on a hill behind the building. Sohan immediately established martial law in Perry County.

The courts reopened. However, in a report to General Hill, Captain Sohan noted that Judge Lilly, in charging the jury, did not seem to take murder seriously.

Captain Sohan began working with the citizens who wanted to see law and order re-established. His troops began rounding up those who participated in the war. The civil authorities charged them with various crimes, including murder.

Captain Sohan organized a company of State Militia, known as the Home Guard, before he and his troops departed Hazard. However, nearly all of the men who enlisted had been involved in the French-Eversole battles. Therefore, as soon as Sohan and his men left, the feud resumed.

Chapter 8

The Battle of Hazard

By 1889, Tom Smith's outlaw reputation had spread throughout southeastern Kentucky. An election that year brought changes in courthouse leadership that diminished Fult French's influence. The courthouse changes also led to a group of concerned citizens in Hazard and Perry County demanding that Tom Smith be brought to justice.

A Perry County Grand Jury was formed in the fall of 1889. It heard a number of witnesses testify about the murders and attempted murders in which Smith was said to have been involved. The grand jury handed down several indictments. The people in Hazard and Perry County were delighted. Bad Tom Smith would finally be brought to justice.

Their joy was short-lived, however. Just before the court was to render its final decision on Tom and the other outlaws, on the night of the Fourth of July, 1890, Bad Tom and members of the Fult French gang set fire to the Perry County Courthouse. The flames leveled the building, destroying all of Bad Tom Smith's criminal records. Not surprisingly, an investigation determined that the fire was an act of arson. Smith was indicted for the fire, but was not tried, due to a lack of evidence. Many people said the courthouse was so riddled with bullet holes that it wouldn't hold corn shucks and that Bad Tom had done the town a favor by burning it down.

By now, Bad Tom Smith was a legend in southeastern Kentucky. He reached the height of power when the courthouse was torched. Smith and the Fult French gang now had Hazard and Perry County under their complete control. Some families were so afraid they packed up and moved out of the county. Judge Josiah Combs and his family were among them.

As the courthouse lay in charred ruins, the new Perry County administration—elected on a platform of ending violence in the county—now had to find new space. The county judge who had openly led the battle to put Bad Tom Smith at the end of a noose, or at least behind bars, now feared Smith would come after him. The courtroom was moved to temporary quarters until a new courthouse could be built. Judge Ed Hensley quit showing up for court. He was so afraid that Bad Tom or another member of the Fult French gang would kill him that he began disguising himself as a woman and mostly staying indoors.

The new Perry County Circuit Clerk, elected on the reform ticket, was Ira Davidson, Joe Eversole's brother-in-law. He had signed Bad Tom Smith's marriage license. Davidson had been unsuccessful in bringing Bad Tom to justice. Now he feared for his life. Bad Tom had openly threatened him. Davidson rounded up his family and left town.

Bad Tom Smith and the Fult French gang also threatened the Perry County Superintendent of Schools, Abner Eversole. Eversole took the threat seriously and fled. All the members of the newly elected county reform administration and many members of the Eversole clan were intimidated into leaving the county.

One member of the Eversole forces let it be known throughout the county that he was not leaving. Robin Cornett told everyone he met, "This is my home and I'm not letting a bunch of cowardly bastards make me abandon it."

Cornett's words got back to Bad Tom Smith, who told all those within earshot, "Who the hell does Cornett think he is? I'll take care of him."

Cornett owned a small farm near Hazard where he eked out a living. During the winter, he did some logging. One crisp morning he and his younger brother went out to cut oats. When they discovered that the grain was not yet ripe enough, they moved into the woods to peel logs. Robin felled a tree across a ravine. He jumped up on the trunk, ax in hand. Shots from the bushes struck him and he fell dead on the log. His little brother ran and managed to escape. Bad Tom, Jesse Morgan, and Bob Prophet had gunned Cornett down from ambush just two days after his reckless statement.

Only a few local government officials and officeholders had not left Perry County by this time. Those remaining included Circuit Judge William Hurst of Wolfe County, who was brought in as a special judge. A tent behind the rubble of the burned courthouse served as a temporary location for county business. Judge Hurst put together a Perry County Grand Jury. After hearing testimony, it returned a murder indictment against Bad Tom Smith for the killing of Robin Cornett.

"I'm glad you gentlemen had the guts to return this indictment against Tom Smith. This county has got to do something with this rattlesnake," Judge Hurst told the grand jurors. "I'm going over to the marshal's office to give him the indictment and have Smith arrested."

The judge crossed the street to the temporary marshal's office and jail that had been erected following the courthouse fire. "A.G., the County Grand Jury has just returned a murder indictment against Tom Smith! Arrest him and bring him in for trial."

Marshall A.G. Duff looked at the paper, then looked up at Hurst. "Do you think I'm crazy? I know it's my job, but bringing Tom Smith in on a murder charge would be like committing suicide! Smith doesn't like me anyway and doesn't need much of an excuse to kill me."

Judge Hurst threw up his hands, looked down at the ground, and then walked out of the marshal's office without another word.

No one attempted to arrest Bad Tom. He ignored the indictment and the orders to appear in court. No one doubted that the Fult French forces completely dominated Perry County.

Word soon reached the Eversole camp that Marshal Duff was afraid to arrest Bad Tom Smith. The Eversoles decided they were going to see justice done, even if they had to do it themselves. Their forces flooded into Hazard. When the French clan heard what was going on, they sent a large group of men in also.

The French forces decided that the courts were against them. Therefore, they would shut down the court system and rule Hazard by force. On the other side, the Eversoles were determined that Bad

Tom Smith and the Fult French gang had to pay for their many and terrible offenses.

Hazard was crowded, but the residents not already scared out of the county, and who were not members of either side, went home and stayed inside. Five hours passed peacefully. The tension, however, was so thick it could be cut with a knife. But no fight had started; no shots had been fired. Neither side seemed eager to start the anticipated battle. This peace did not last long, however.

Many of the men from both sides did some heavy drinking. The French forces and the members of the Eversole clan had been drinking most of the day. One of the Eversole men, and Henry Davidson, a member of the French gang, spotted a barrel of applejack sitting on the sidewalk near the town barber shop and Wesley Whitaker's place at the same time.

Whitaker, the Eversole man, reached down to pick up the barrel. Davidson yelled, "What the hell you think you are going to do with that applejack, you Eversole bastard?"

"I'm going to drink the damn stuff, and you and the rest of your French sons-a-bitches are not going to stop me," Whitaker yelled back.

Whitaker drew his gun. Before he could fire, Davidson entered the nearby home of Jesse Fields. When Davidson got inside the house, he quickly pulled a gun and shot at Whitaker, who returned the fire. The two were drunk and both missed. However, their gunfire put an end to five hours of peaceful tension.

The French and Eversole forces pitched a full-scale gun battle.

James Davidson led a contingent of Eversole forces. French's men, who were numerous and had plenty of ammunition, marched into Hazard from nearby Lotts Creek, arriving at one o'clock Wednesday morning. They could be heard above the noise of their Winchesters, shouting, "Hurrah for Fult French! He is our king and we will follow him to hell." The gunfire continued until two o'clock that afternoon, the second day of the Perry County Circuit Court's session. Everything that moved became a target. Some members of the Eversole group were badly wounded, needing medical help. Ambrose Amburgy, whom Bad Tom had wounded earlier, was back in good health, leading the Eversole forces. He noticed that Whitaker had sobered up somewhat. He asked him, "Do you know where we can find a doctor to patch up the boys? I'm afraid some of them might die if we don't get them some help."

Whitaker said, "The only doctor that Fult French don't control is Dr. Dan F. Hamilton over in Leslie County, at Frew on Wooten's Creek, near Farler. You've got to cross three mountains to get to his house. The good doctor isn't swayed by either side. He is a dedicated fair man."

Amburgy said, "Well, get on your horse and go get him right now. Sneak out the back. Don't let them French bastards see you."

It had been dark about four hours by the time Whitaker and Dr. Hamilton came into the back of the building where most of the Eversole forces were holed up.

"Good to see you, Doc," Amburgy said. I didn't know you were a doctor. I thought you were a school teacher."

"I used to be a teacher, but the people here need doctors more than they do teachers! I went home to Virginia in order to study medicine, and then came back. By the way, do you know who signed my teaching certificate before I started teaching up on Cutshin?"

With a puzzled look on his face, Amburgy looked at Hamilton. "No, Doc, I don't."

"It was Joe Eversole and Fult French," Hamilton said.

Amburgy just shook his head. "Things have shore changed now, hain't they Doc?"

"They sure have, Mr. Amburgy."

When darkness covered the valley, reinforcements sneaked into the French camp. The Eversoles were badly outnumbered but they did not give up. The shooting continued for eighteen hours.

The Eversoles finally ran out of ammunition and were forced to leave town.

More than two thousand shots were fired during the battle, but only two men were killed, Jake McKnight and Ed Campbell, both on the Eversole side. Bad Tom Smith shot McKnight. The French forces took no casualties in what has become known as the Battle of Hazard. It was an outright victory for the French forces. The people not friendly to them were thoroughly terrified.

The French forces threatened to kill Circuit Judge W.L. Hurst if he did not leave Hazard within five minutes. Hurst, who had tried his best to clean up Perry County, rode out of town in well under the allotted time.

Word of the battle in Hazard reached Governor Buckner in

Frankfort. Greatly perturbed, he immediately dispatched General Sam Hill and a compliment of State Militia troops to Hazard to assess the situation. After arriving in Perry County two weeks later, General Hill sent Governor Buckner a dispatch that described Hazard as a dirty, shabby excuse for a town. He wrote that what little town was left had been shot to pieces. Since he and the troops had arrived, some of the people who had left because of the violence were returning. A few had already started repairing and rebuilding their homes and businesses.

General Hill's troops began rounding up men suspected of crimes during the recent battle. One of those taken into custody was Bad Tom Smith. He was indicted on a first degree murder charge in connection with the shooting death of Jake McKnight. Authorities decided to move Smith's trial out of Perry County, fearing the French forces still could intimidate jury members there.

Smith's trial was moved to Pineville in Bell County, Kentucky. When the outlaw arrived, the street to the courthouse was lined with people wanting to see him taken to the Bell County Jail, where he was held during the trial. When the verdict was returned, Bad Tom Smith was found guilty of first degree murder and sentenced to life in prison.

Fult French obtained the best lawyer money could buy for Smith. He appealed the case to the Kentucky Court of Appeals, which reversed the conviction. Smith's attorney claimed there was no evidence that he had killed Jake McKnight, or anyone else, in the several hours of gunfire during the Battle of Hazard. Bad Tom was never tried again on that charge.

General Hill's troops arrested twelve other men who had been involved in the battle. One of them was Joe Davidson, a French supporter who had boasted that there were not enough soldiers in Perry County to take him. One night, Captain Gaither heard that Davidson was at his home a short distance from Hazard. He sent a guard named Gaines to arrest him. Arriving at the house, Gaines saw Davidson through a crack in the wall and called on him to surrender. Davidson reached for his gun when Gaines kicked in the door. But Gaines already had his pistol aimed at Davidson. He ordered the outlaw to raise his hands. Davidson is quoted as saying, "I will surrender to the soldiers, but no sheriff can take me." When he got outside and discovered there were no soldiers accompanying Gaines, he became extremely angry and frustrated. A single man had bluffed him and taken him into custody.

Davidson is said to have been the most hardened of the twelve arrested. He was thirty-two, a large raw-boned man. Davidson was charged with murder in three indictments and placed under indictment on sixty-four additional charges. Two years earlier, he had shot a little girl in the brain, killing her instantly. Asked why he did it, Davidson said, "I had just bought a new pistol. I wanted to try it out and the little girl was the first living thing I saw." His companions were shocked and repulsed by what he did. They nearly killed him on the street.

Captain Gaither and his troops arrested Davidson and the eleven other men and took them to Winchester, Kentucky in Clark County, where they were incarcerated in the same room, on September 2,

1890. Seven of the men were from the Eversole faction, including brothers George and John Eversole. Five came from the French faction, including Fult French. Captain Gaither, commander of the troops sent to Perry County, arrived in Winchester to take charge of sixteen prisoners, four of whom had been convicted for felonies and sentenced to the penitentiary. The other prisoners included Jesse Fields, William B. Smith, Job Jones, Green Morris, Frank Polly, Joe Rawlins, Ed Combs, and Wes Whitaker.

Henry Fugate, a seventeen-year-old boy, was among them. Along with his brother Zack, he had waylaid Constable Allen in Perry County in July, 1889, and killed him. Allen had Buck, another Fugate brother, under arrest and was conducting him to the Perry County Jail in Hazard when Henry Fugate killed him. All the prisoners initially got away. Most of them, including Zack, got away clean, but Buck and Henry Fugate were soon re-arrested. They, and all those who did escape, were soldiers in the French and Eversole factions, and all had been charged with murder.

After a great deal of pleading to the authorities, a reporter from the Big Stone Post newspaper in Big Stone Gap, Virginia, interviewed the Eversole brothers and Fult French. Even though they were in the same room, the men were peaceful. The Eversole brothers and French had long discussions on how to get the charges against them dismissed. The men, who had been bitter enemies to the point of trying to kill each other, now became friends, plotting to beat the legal system. They had totally disregarded the law in Perry County, but now both sides were disarmed, facing serious charges.

Eversole told the reporter that he had nothing to do with the killings of Campbell and McKnight, whom he said were his friends. He added that Judge Lilly was holding him without bail to absolve himself from accusations of being too lenient. French was so ill he had to have the services of a physician.

Joe Davidson was the first of the twelve to stand trial. People from Perry and the surrounding counties filled the Clark County Courtroom. Davidson was charged with killing Ed Campbell. Campbell had fired some shots from Graveyard Hill in Hazard toward the county jail building, which was near the courthouse and Davidson's saloon. Davidson responded by grabbing his Winchester and shooting Campbell, who was standing on the hill waving his pistol. Davidson's defense claimed that their client's brother was a prisoner in the jail, and that Davidson was trying to protect him.

W.P. Bentley opened the case for the Commonwealth. He gave an account of the rise and progress of the feud in which so much blood had been shed, with whole counties terrorized for years. He had been present at the time of the fight and thus was able to give a graphic description of the entire scene. Bentley said the prisoner was never in danger, and that Joe Davidson could not have even known his brother was an inmate of the jail at that time. Therefore, the killing could not have been in his defense. W.P. Bentley claimed that Davidson ran a saloon in open violation of the law, and that the liquor dispensed over his bar had had much to do with inflaming the already heated passions of the factions.

Perry County Judge R.F. Fields accompanied the prisoners to

Winchester. His brother, Jesse Fields, was one of the incarcerated men. After being in jail for several weeks, each of the twelve prisoners demanded examining trials. After posting bail, they were allowed to return to their homes in Perry County.

Judge Josiah Combs, who left Perry County during the height of the feud, returned to his home in Hazard along with many other residents following the arrests of Bad Tom Smith, Fult French, the Eversole brothers, and many of their followers. With only one exception, Hazard and Perry County had been peaceful following the many arrests by the troops ordered in by the governor. Jesse Fields, a French follower, and some of the Eversole faction got into a shootout on Hazard's Main Street. Fields and some of the Eversole followers were wounded, and a black bystander was killed by a stray bullet.

Judge Combs had secretly returned to his home in Hazard on several occasions. On one clandestine visit, someone opened fire as Combs entered his house. Combs managed to get in without injury, but his front door looked like Swiss cheese. The Judge had miscalculated about safely returning home.

Many of his friends and associates tried to persuade him to stay away from Perry County, especially after this assassination attempt. Combs did not listen. In 1894, he came back to Hazard with his son-in-law, Ira Davidson, who had also fled Perry County during the feud. Both had been living in Laurel County near London, Kentucky.

On the morning following the arrival of Combs in Hazard, a neighbor came and told him that something was wrong with his mowing machine. A nearby fenced lot, full of tall corn and thick, bushy weeds, provided cover for several assassins. As Combs stooped over to examine the mower, the men in the weeds opened fire. The judge, who was hit just below the heart, staggered toward his house. Bystanders picked Combs up, carried him into his house, and laid him on a pallet. The son-in-law ran around the house, came in the back door, and held the judge's hand. Combs died within minutes. Witnesses said that three men fled the weedy lot and headed for the North Fork of the Kentucky River. Strangely, they were white men made up in blackface.

By the time a posse could be rounded up and organized, the assassins had a big head start. The posse finally spotted the three killers and exchanged gunfire with them. One assassin and one posse member were wounded. A running gun battle continued until the three fleeing men disappeared into the dense mountain forests. The posse recognized the three men as Joe Adkins, Jesse Fields, and Boone Frazier. Adkins, they said, had probably fired the shot that killed Judge Josiah Combs. The three men had long served the French faction; all were indicted. Adkins and Fields were arrested; Frazier was never captured.

Chapter 9

Tom Helps Start a Church

When growing up, Emaline Combs had gone to church with her family every time there was a local church service. While there were no churches in Hazard, occasionally a preacher held a service at the schoolhouse in town. There were a few churches in some of the rural areas of Perry County. Harry Caudill writes in his book, *Night Comes to the Cumberlands*, that court records indicate that as many people showed up for religious services to harass the preacher as to worship God. He tells the story about a big strong mountaineer named George Johnson who had been a renowned fighter before he got saved at a small weather -beaten church on Grapevine Creek in Perry County. After he got religion, Johnson was in attendance at every service held in the building. During one service on a warm Sunday morning, six rowdy young men in the community appeared outside the open door of the church building. They began to repeat every word the preacher said and the minister was confused and had trouble continuing. Finally he asked all those in attendance to bow their heads in "a moment of silent prayer after which we will adjourn the services for a few minutes while Brother George Johnson knocks hell out of 'em for God."

As the children grew older, the Tom Smith family did not attend church services. Emma tried to talk Tom into going, but he always refused. Finally, Emma decided she would go to church without him. Emma, Matilda, Bud, Maggie, John, and Cody started attending occasional Baptist services held in the schoolhouse. Their daughter, Matilda (Tildy), in not too many years would be a teenager. Emma believed that exposure to church people and Bible preaching was helping her and the five children, especially since their father was getting a reputation as a "bad" man.

One day in July of 1892, Emma and the children were getting ready for church. Tom shocked his wife. "Emma, is it all right if I go to church with you and the children this morning?"

"Tom Smith, I've been asking you to go to church with us for quite a while. Tildy was just a baby when I started going, and you didn't want anything to do with it."

"Are you ashamed to be seen with me in church?"

"No, Tom. I'm not ashamed to be seen with you anywhere. And if you want to go, put on some of your best clothes, and hurry or we'll be late."

Tom quickly donned his one good suit. The family went together to the church for the first time ever. After the service, Emma noticed Tom was frowning.

"What's wrong, Tom?"

"Oh, I don't know. I really didn't like that preacher, and them people don't know how to sing. Some of the people there stared a hole through me like I had leprosy or something. Is there another church we could go to?"

"I overheard one of the ladies at church today saying that a traveling Presbyterian preacher is trying to start a church in Hazard," Emma said.

"What's his name?"

"The lady said it was Grant. No, that's not it. Guerrant, I think she said. Edward Guerrant. He's from away. They say he's an evangelist who is going to hold a revival in Hazard to stir up some interest in starting a Presbyterian Church. I hear that this preacher has even written a book called *Bloody Breathitt*. He should be interesting."

"Emma, did they say when the revival is going to be? I haven't been to an old time revival since I was a little boy. The singing is usually really good at revivals."

"Well, I think she said August 14th. That's a Sunday. The revival is going to run for two weeks."

"Let's go one or two times anyway, Emma. We can take the children with us."

"All right, Tom. Anything to get you to church."

In the summer of 1892, the Reverend Doctor Guerrant rode from Jackson, some thirty-five miles up the North Fork of the Kentucky River, to Hazard to hold a revival. He normally used a large tent, but the road between Jackson and Hazard was so rough it would be difficult to haul the tent for thirty-five miles. The minister later described the Perry County seat as consisting of "a courthouse, a jail, four stores, and seventeen families."

Tom and his family did not go to the Baptist church Emma and the children had been attending. Emma didn't want to offend Tom and hoped that perhaps the Presbyterian minister could reach him. On Sunday, August 14th, Tom, Emma, and all five children walked to the new Perry County Courthouse, where the revival was being held.

Tildy's eyes almost popped out! She had never seen anything like this. "Mama, is this where we are going to start going to church?"

"No, darling, they are only going to have church here for two weeks. This is called a revival."

"That's a funny word, Mama. I'm glad Papa came with us."

"I am too, darling."

Tom and his family sat down on one of the seats near the back of the courtroom. The revival began at ten o'clock in the morning and the first session would end at two o'clock in the afternoon. The Smiths arrived fifteen minutes early and the courtroom was about half full. Then, people started pouring in. By the time the service got underway there were only a few empty places.

Promptly at nine o'clock, Reverend Guerrant stepped behind the lectern. "Ladies and gentlemen, I know the seats in the courtroom are not the most comfortable in the world, but the Gospel is not bound to circular pews and cushioned seats. 'God's first temple' is greater and grander than all abbeys and cathedrals. It is wide as the earth, and its dome is lit with the stars!"

Reverend Guerrant introduced two men as soloists. They sang hymns *a cappella*. One of them led the congregation in two hymns he lined out in a style used by the Old Regular Baptists. This was necessary; not only were there no hymn books, but most of those present could not have read them anyhow.

Following the music service and a long prayer, Reverend Guerrant stood behind the lectern and began his message. His preaching style was animated; it quickly led him from behind the speaker's stand. He waved his arms and Bible, walking quickly back and forth in front of the crowd, raising his voice, lowering it, then raising it again. Even when his voice was low, Reverend Guerrant had the ability to project so that it could be heard throughout the room.

For four hours, the people listened to Reverend Guerrant preach a solid Christian message of God's salvation for man through the death of Jesus Christ on the cross. Many people murmured and whispered, saying they had never heard about Jesus' death for their sins.

Following the service, Guerrant gave an invitation message. He asked those who wanted to repent of their sins and to accept the salvation Jesus offered through His death to come forward. Ten people came and made confessions of faith that first day. Tom and his family were not among them.

The long service ended and the crowd dispersed. Tom, Emma, and the children were walking home when Emma said, "What did you think of the preacher, Tom?"

"I liked him! He sounded like an intelligent man. Bout all the preachers that I've heard was uneducated. Dr. Guerrant could talk so as people like me could understand his message. He was a medical doctor first, and then he became an evangelist. That's a rare combination! You know, I almost went up front with those other people. There was something urging me to, but I just didn't."

Matilda looked at her father. "Papa, can we come back to the revival? I liked it there."

Tom looked at his daughter with a tear welling up in his eye. "Yes, Tildy, we will go back."

Emma said, "Oh, Tom, what day do you want to go?"

"Well, we could go the last day he's here. Is that all right?"

"That would be perfect."

Emma knew about all the activities her husband had been involved in with the Fult French gang over the last several years. She didn't approve of them. She knew he was called "Bad Tom" around Hazard. She hoped that if Tom got involved in church, if he got "saved," maybe he would change. She had faith. Now, it appeared God might be answering her prayers.

Reverend Guerrant watched the crowd leaving the courtroom. It had been a wonderful service, he decided, but it would have been better if more than ten souls had come forward for salvation.

One of the townspeople at the service, Bill Baker, the lying man who had worked in Fult French's store, stayed in the tent until the crowd left, then walked up front to talk to Reverend Guerrant. Baker was the one who told Joe Eversole he had heard French planning to kill him, which triggered the feud between the two families.

Baker said, "Reverend, I'm Bill Baker. I really enjoyed your sermon today."

"Thank you, Mr. Baker. Did you wish to speak to me about something?" Guerrant said.

"Yes sir, I do. In the back of the courtroom, did you notice a man with a mustache? He was with a woman and a young girl about eleven or twelve years old. There were also four smaller children."

"No, sir. I didn't notice them. There were a lot of people here."

"Well, Reverend, that man is well known in this community. People call him Bad Tom Smith."

"How did he get the name 'Bad,' Mr. Baker?"

"You've heard of the French-Eversole Feud?"

"Yes, I have."

"Bad Tom Smith is the leader of the French gang. He is said to have killed three or four people, including Joe Eversole, the head of the Eversole family. Tom has everybody in this community scared to death. Every time he's charged with a crime, whether it be robbery or murder, Fult French gets him off. Many say Bad Tom was behind burning the courthouse down. I don't understand what a man like that was doing with his family at a preaching service."

"Mr. Baker, if this Bad Tom Smith is the desperado you depict, then this is the very place he needs to be. People like that need to hear God's word. No matter what Tom Smith has done, he can be saved. Even the Apostle Paul was feared by the early Christians because he persecuted them. But he became the greatest Christian leader in history, other than Jesus himself. If this Bad Tom Smith and his family want to come back to our revival, they will be most welcome."

"Well, Reverend, I thought that you needed to know."

"Thank you, Mr. Baker." Baker walked out of the courtroom with a puzzled look. Guerrant had not reacted at all as he had expected.

Rev. Dr. Guerrant immediately got on his knees and prayed a

long prayer for Bad Tom Smith and his family.

August 28th was the last session of Reverend Guerrant's revival in Hazard. Emma had been busy the past two weeks with household duties and taking care of Tom's needs. Tom stayed busy doing the various tasks Fult French assigned.

The adult Smiths had not discussed the single revival service they had attended. However, Tildy thought about it constantly. She reminded her parents about their promise to go back to the revival. She mentioned it at breakfast that Sunday morning. Emma said, "Of course we are going. Daddy promised."

"Yes, Emma. Thank you Tildy for reminding us."

The Smith family again walked to the courthouse. They eagerly entered the courtroom. This time they sat closer to the front. By the time the service started the room was packed. There was not an empty space anywhere. The service consisted of the traditional singing by the soloists and the congregation. In the mountains of Kentucky, the typical revival services of that day were conducted without musical instruments. Organs and pianos were too heavy to haul from one site to another. The song leader would line out the words from a hymn book because a large number of the attendees could not read or write. The Old Regular Baptist churches in the mountains of Kentucky still use this method today. However, the lining of songs by the Old Regular Baptists uses a mournful cadence that has been described in a documentary filmed by John Cohen in the early 1960s as *That High Lonesome Sound*. That is the name of the documentary filmed in Hazard and Perry County. The lining of songs by the Presbyterians was in a natural cadence.

Reverend Guerrant's sermon differed a great deal from the one they had heard two weeks earlier.

However, the theme of salvation through Jesus' death on the cross was the same. Again, Guerrant issued an altar call as he ended the sermon. Tom, Emma, and Tildy again did not go forward. Before dismissing the crowd with a prayer, Guerrant said, "I have an announcement to make. There is no Presbyterian Church in Hazard or in all of Perry County. I am interested in starting one. I would like to invite those who would like to be a part of starting a new church to join me at six o'clock Wednesday evening in the dining room of the Palace Hotel, where we will discuss starting a Presbyterian Church in Hazard. Again, the time is six o'clock Wednesday evening in the dining room of the Palace Hotel." Reverend Guerrant then closed the service in prayer and the crowd started leaving.

During the service, the evangelist remembered the description of Tom Smith and his family that Bill Baker had given him. He had been looking for the Smith family at each service the past two weeks. The minister was pleased when he spotted the Smiths in the crowd today. He had been hopeful they would respond to the invitation, and was disheartened when they did not. He noticed them talking to each other as they left the courtroom.

"Tom, what did you think of the Reverend's sermon this time?"

"I think this Guerrant man is one of the most sensible men I've ever heard talk, Emma. Do you want to go to that meeting at the hotel on Wednesday?"

"Oh, Tom, I'd love to."

"Good. Then it's settled. We'll go. Tildy can look after the other children."

At 5:30 Wednesday evening, August 31, 1892, in the dining room of the Palace Hotel, Rev. Dr. Guerrant had just arrived and was scurrying around trying to make sure there would be enough chairs for those he expected to attend the church organizational meeting. By 5:45, ten people had arrived. Five minutes later he was somewhat shocked to see Tom Smith and his wife Emma walk in. Guerrant walked up to the couple and introduced himself. "I'm Reverend Edward Guerrant, and who would you be?"

"We know who you are preacher; we attended your revival twice. I'm Tom Smith and this is my wife, Emaline. Just call her Emma."

"It is good to have you here, Mr. and Mrs. Smith. Here are two seats you can use." Guerrant directed Tom and Emma to two empty straight-back chairs. As they sat down, Tom told Guerrant, "Reverend, I've heard several preachers in my time, and you make the most sense of anyone I've heard. That's why we are here this evening."

"I'm glad you came," Guerrant said. Then he asked, "Mr. Smith, do you know if you are related to Reverend Thomas Smith who came to the Cranbury, New Jersey First Presbyterian Church in 1762?"

"Well, Reverend, my grandfather was a preacher, but his name was Richard, same as my father. Also, my uncle is a preacher. His name is Thomas, but he's a Kelly, and all of them are Baptists. Anyway, Kentucky is where we all live. Don't know nothing about any of my people being from New Jersey."

"Well Mr. Smith, it's a long way from New Jersey to Kentucky.

Anyhow, this particular Thomas Smith was called as pastor to the church in Cranbury in 1762. The congregation had been started nineteen years before in 1743, and had not done too well. They had used supply preachers until installing Reverend Thomas Smith as pastor. After the arrival of Minister Smith, the church formed eight other Presbyterian congregations. During a period of 130 years between 1762 and 1892, the Cranbury Church was without a pastor for only two and a half years."

Bad Tom listened to Guerrant's remarkable story and then replied, "Preacher, I don't know if I'm kin to that fellow or not. It would be nice to be. Do you think Hazard is a good place for a Presbyterian Church?"

"With the help of people like you, Mr. Smith, I have very high expectations for a new church here."

By the time the meeting got underway at six o'clock, thirty-eight people were in attendance. Guerrant told the crowd that if they constituted a congregation, the Presbyterian Church would send them a preacher at least once a month until they could get a permanent pastor. The minister also said that the Hazard community would need to find a temporary place to worship until a church building could be constructed.

Near the end of the meeting, Guerrant passed around a paper for those present to sign to constitute a church. Thirty-five of the thirty-eight people there signed, including Emaline and Tom Smith. Thus, they became supporters of what was to be the First Presbyterian Church of Hazard.

Chapter 10

Marital Problems

The news spread around Hazard like a wildfire! Bad Tom Smith had found religion. He was one of a group of people who had organized a Presbyterian Church in Hazard. Many people thought it was sacrilegious. How dare a man who had terrorized the town claim he was a Christian and start going to church! There were others, although a minority, who thought Tom's newfound religion was genuine, and hoped that his "bad" days were behind him.

The new Presbyterian Church started meeting in an abandoned store building. Ironically, the store's former owner had been one of the people intimidated by Fult French, who had fled for his life along with his family, taking only what they could stuff into their saddle bags on their horses. That occurred after the Fult French forces led by Tom Smith had taken control of Hazard.

Tom, Emma, and their five children attended each Sunday there was a service. Emaline, a Combs before marriage, encouraged her parents to attend. At first the church held services only once a month, when a traveling preacher could preside. Then, the congregation organized a Sabbath School that met every Sunday, with church members teaching Sabbath School lessons. Preaching services, however, were still held only once a month. The congregation initiated a building program to raise money for the construction of a new church building.

Tom settled down, very nearly becoming a respectable citizen. He was at church every Sunday. One day, as he walked down Main Street, he ran into George Whitaker, one of his fellow church members. George walked up and said, "Well pawn my word and honor if it hain't Tom Smith. Tom, it's shore you hain't it. I'd know ye in Shanghai with yore under jaw shot off!"

Tom didn't know what to make of this greeting, but was glad people were happy to see him now. He liked the new respectability that his association with the church had brought. Emma also liked it. She began to hope the worst days of her marriage to Tom were over.

Tom was beginning to gain some respect in Hazard, but he was still on the Fult French payroll. As of the spring of 1893, Tom had not been to the Fult French headquarters for several months. He never told Emma that he had quit the French forces, but she erroneously believed he had.

Tom had become very active in the Presbyterian congregation. He was paying more attention to Emma and the children, and had become an attentive, caring husband and father. Also, Emma learned she was pregnant again. Then a man arrived at their home one day and said, "Tom, Mr. French wants to see you right away. He's got a job for you."

"All right, I'll be ready as soon as I can saddle up my horse," Tom said. He walked toward the barn. Emma ran after him.

"Tom, I thought you were through with Fult French. I don't want you to go."

"Emma, I have to. Where do you think I've been getting the money to pay the rent and buy food and clothes? Fult has been good to me. If he needs me, I owe it to him to help." As her husband rode toward the French stronghold, Emma cried.

Tom began to spend more and more time at the French headquarters and less time at home. His church attendance became sporadic. He still occasionally attended with his family, but then might miss two or three Sundays at a time. Finally, he dropped out altogether.

Emma never knew when Tom might show up. He would be gone days at a time and then walk in unannounced. One day when he showed up, he noticed Susan Eversole sitting in the front room, talking with Emma. It naturally upset Tom that the widow of a man he had killed was visiting, but he did not make a scene. With a strained smile he looked at the visitor. "Mrs. Eversole, how are you doing today?"

With an equally strained smile Susan Eversole stared at Tom. "I am all right, Mr. Smith. I was just visiting my cousin, Emaline. I'd better be going now." She stood. "We'll have to get together again. Goodbye, Emaline. Goodbye, Mr. Smith." She walked to the door, opened it, and left, closing the door with the slightest slam.

"What in the world was that all about, Emma?" Tom asked.

"It's just what she said it was Tom, a visit from a cousin. She's kin to me on my daddy's side," Emma told Tom.

Tom gave Emma a stern look. "I don't want that woman coming in my house. I don't care if she is your cousin. I work for Fult French and he's at war with her husband's family."

Emma flared back, "Her dead husband, you mean. Dead because you murdered him! Why did you have to kill him?"

"You don't seem to understand that we are in a war. Some of Fult French's people have been killed by the Eversoles too. For heaven's sake, Emma, they have tried to kill me. Is this the type of people you want coming into our house?"

With fire in her eyes, she shouted, "Yes, I'd rather have them in my house than those filthy French men you ride with. They are as low as snakes."

Tom did not answer. He headed for the front door, steaming. Tom walked outside, slamming the door hard enough to shake the house. He got on his horse and rode back to the French stronghold, where he stayed a couple of days.

Fult French said, "What's wrong with you, Tom? You look like you've lost your last friend."

"Fult, I think I might have lost Emma. I'm crazy about her, but she's been doing some strange things lately. I don't think my woman feels the same way about me as when we got hitched." He didn't tell Fult about Susan Eversole's visit.

"Tom, women go through stages sometimes. Why don't you go back home and try to make up with her?"

"I think I will, Fult. I sure don't want to lose her."

Tom left the big house where the French forces were living and rode home. When he walked in, Susan Eversole and several Eversole women were sitting in his front room, talking with Emma. Tom glared at Emma with daggers in his eyes. "You ain't nothing but a damn Eversole woman. If you like them so much, let them take care of you and the younguns. I won't be back."

He walked out, slammed the door, got on his horse, and rode to the French headquarters.

Tom lived at the French house with several other hired men for a few months. Over the last several weeks, there had been no assignments. The Eversole forces had dwindled to a handful of men. As a result, there had been none of the familiar ambushes that had marked the height of the French-Eversole Feud.

On a beautiful, quiet morning in the early fall of 1893, Fult French called his men together. His forces were also not nearly as large as they had been at the height of the feud. Only about thirty men still worked for him.

"Boys, I have some good news and some bad news for you," French said. "You have probably noticed that I haven't given you anything to do lately. I'm told the Eversoles only have six or seven outsiders still working for them. They haven't bothered us in a while. I guess you could say the war is over. That's the good news! Now comes the bad news. I'm going to have to let you boys go. I can't keep paying you when I don't have anything for you to do. You boys have been of great service to me, especially you, Tom. But I can't keep paying you. I'll give each of you ten dollars to help you get settled."

French gave each man a ten-dollar bill, then dismissed them.

They dutifully gathered their belongings, then drifted away. Tom had not given any thought as to what to do once the feud was over. He needed to sort things out. He didn't want to go back home to Emma, Tildy, and the other children. Tom couldn't stand the thought of Emma's betrayal, messing around with them Eversoles.

Tom thought back to his childhood. He used to enjoy playing on the Combs farm at Quicksand, Kentucky with his second cousin, Breck. He had always enjoyed going there! Breck's parents had treated him just like one of their sons. Breck, he had heard, had moved to Jackson and was now the Breathitt County Sheriff. Tom decided to go to Jackson. A change of scenery would be good for him!

Chapter 11

On to Breathitt County

Fult French closed his store in Hazard and opened a new one on Lost Creek in Breathitt County. On February 3, 1887, while visiting Louisville to buy goods for his new store, French shared a drink with a reporter for the *Pittsburgh Dispatch*. "Owing to this feud," he said, "I have left Perry County forever. It wasn't because I was afraid of losing my life. I went away from there because my expenses were so heavy that it was about to take everything I had to pay them. I suppose I was what would be called a wealthy man in the mountains. When things grew pretty warm, I was compelled to hire a bodyguard, and I had to make it a strong one, too, to prevent my being overpowered by the other side. At one time I had thirty men in my employ and I was paying each of them fifty dollars a month, and furnishing them with rations. Considering all things, they cost me two thousand dollars a month. I did not keep that many long, but I nearly always had several to whom I paid salaries to protect me. I provided them with arms also. I have bought during the trouble not less than one hundred and sixty Winchester rifles, besides revolvers and cartridges."

"At what cost would you place the total cost of the feud to you?" the reporter asked.

French replied, "I have not kept an exact account of the items, but I think I can make a close estimate. I have paid out in money on account of the feud twenty thousand dollars. I have hundreds of friends who are ready to fight for me, but as I am considered the leader I am expected to foot all the bills. I am bled greatly in the way of loans which are never paid."

Because he continued to fear assassination by the Eversole forces, French still employed a few of his troops, headquartered out of his new home in Breathitt County.

At the French house, Tom gathered the belongings he had kept. Basically, there were a few changes of clothes, underwear, socks, and other things. The items were tied in a blanket and fastened on the back of his saddle. Tom then got on his horse and headed toward Jackson.

Jackson, the Breathitt County seat, was a wide-open town known for whiskey, loose women, and violence. There had been so many killings in Jackson, and elsewhere in the county, that the area had received the nickname of "Bloody Breathitt." This now sounded appealing to Tom. He had grown comfortable with a criminal lifestyle during the French-Eversole Feud. Now that it was over and Emma had—in his mind—betrayed him, Hazard and Perry County held no allure.

The town of Jackson wanted to rid itself of the violent image that appealed to people like Tom. The Lexington and Eastern Railroad had arrived two years earlier. Since its arrival, Jackson's population had increased from 200 residents to 2,000. The new brick Breathitt

County Courthouse, completed in 1888, cost the taxpayers $12,000, plus $8,300 for a new jail with jailer's quarters on the same lot.

Tom had intended to go straight to Jackson, but he began to think about his boyhood days with cousin Breck Combs on Quicksand Creek. Along the way, he decided to ride by the South Fork of Quicksand to look around the old Combs place again. Tom knew Breck didn't live there anymore, having moved to Jackson even before becoming high sheriff. Tom just wanted to look the place over again.

The ride from the French stronghold to the South Fork of Quicksand Creek, while not long, was exceedingly dusty. Shortly after Tom started his journey, he noticed a rider coming toward him. When the rider got close enough, he saw that it was a little girl— maybe eight years old—on a mule. The mule was loaded with all types of merchandise—pots and pans, two sacks of potatoes, bags of green beans, leaf lettuce, cabbage, cushaws, muskmelons, and five live chickens tied together. As Tom approached, the little girl moved a little bit to check on some of the goods tied onto her mule. The load shifted, sending the little girl, pots and pans, vegetables, and chickens off the mule. The girl and the merchandise rolled down a hill. The chickens were loose and running wild.

Tom stopped, got off his horse, and tied it to a bush. He walked down the hill.

"Are you hurt?" Tom said.

The child dusted herself. "I'll live, I reckon."

Tears streamed down her face. She had light brown hair, was

about four feet ten inches tall, and wore a brown pair of boys' pants with a large beige-colored blouse that looked like it was made from a feed sack. Tom thought some black printing was located about where the girl tucked the blouse into her pants. Her brogans were worn thin. Tom looked her over; it appeared she was not injured.

"What's your name?"

"Frances Fields. They call me Fran for short. Who are you?"

"My name is Thomas Smith—Tom for short. Where are you going with all that stuff?"

"My mommy wants me to go to Hazard to sell it. This is the road to Hazard, ain't it?"

"Yes, this is the right road, but ain't you a little young to be going to Hazard to sell stuff by yourself? How old are you anyway?"

"I'll be nine years old in five months."

"Well, I've got a little girl a few years older than you, and I wouldn't send her on a pack mule all the way to Hazard selling stuff. It's just too dangerous. I'm on my way to Jackson. Let's get your stuff rounded up and back on that mule. I'll ride to Hazard with you."

Tom rounded up the pots and pans and tied them back on the mule. It took a while to chase down the chickens, tie their feet together, and put them back on the mule. Little Fran gathered up the potatoes and vegetables and Tom tied them to the mule. He lifted Fran back onto her mount, then rode to Hazard with her.

When the pair reached town, Tom told Fran to wait. He went into the saloon to get Thelma, one of the barmaids. Tom told Thelma what had happened and said little Fran needed some help. Thelma went outside, stood beside Fran and her loaded mule, and started shouting at the top of her voice, "All you people come over here. Gather around. This poor youngun might as well be an orphan. Her mother is sick and her daddy's in jail. She's got five brothers and sisters working in the fields, trying to raise some food for the family. The mommy needs some money. That's why this poor youngun is in town today to try to sell the things on the mule. Now, this is good stuff! Little Fran has some vegetables picked at the peak of freshness. There's green beans, not the old flabby kind, but good Kentucky White Runners. She's got rhubarb, cushaws, sweet taters, and leaf lettuce. Look at them new taters. There is not a bad place in any of them. There's five chickens here that are fat and ready to kill and eat. They would make some mighty fine eatin' fer Sunday dinners."

Thelma held up one of the pots.

"Not only does this youngun have the main dish for your Sunday dinner, but she can even sell you a pot to cook it in. Now, you have a chance to help this poor youngun and get some good merchandise at the same time."

A man walked up to Fran and bought one of the sacks of new potatoes. Others came up and started buying the vegetables, pots, and pans. They paid much more than Fran's mother had ever expected to get.

After the last item had been sold, little Fran thanked Thelma. Then, she walked over to Tom. "Mr. Smith, thank you for helping me. I'll never forget you! You are a good man."

Given his well-deserved nickname and reputation, her words

touched his heart. He told Fran, "I want to make sure you get back home with all that money. I'm going to Jackson anyway, so I will ride back with you. Where do you live?"

"Oh, I don't live in Jackson. I live on a farm in Breathitt County not too far from where I had the accident."

"Well, I'll make sure you get there all right. Are you ready to go?"

"Yes, Mr. Smith, I'm ready."

Tom helped her onto the mule, then got on his horse. The two headed for the Breathitt County line. The journey back to where Fran had fallen was uneventful. Tom followed little Fran up a hollow to the small farm where her family lived. The house was a shotgun building of unpainted wood. Someone had nailed a board across the bottom of the open front door. At first puzzled about the board, Tom finally realized that its purpose was to keep the toddlers from going outside when their mother wasn't looking. No grass grew in the front yard. As they rode toward the house, they heard the sound of two barking dogs that turned out to be scraggily hounds. Chickens were pecking in the yard. Tom could tell the family was in the swine business from the stench of a hog pen. He noticed a small hillside garden so steep that watermelons were propped up by rocks to keep them from rolling off the vine.

Tom got off his horse and helped Fran off the mule. She ran to her mommy for a hug. She gave the money to her mother, who was happily surprised by the amount. Fran introduced Tom to everyone else and told them what had happened. Tom noticed the mother looked shocked when she heard his name. He knew that the child did not know who he was, but the adult family members did. They thanked him, but did not invite him inside. Tom quickly said his goodbyes to the Fields family and rode out of the hollow to get back on the trail to Quicksand.

Tom looked over the Combs place where he had often played as a boy. It had not changed much. They had built a new smokehouse in the back, but otherwise it looked the same. After reminiscing for a few minutes, Tom wanted to wash the dust out of his throat. He saw a young man walking down the road. "Mister, where could a body get a good drink of whiskey?"

The young man looked up at Tom. "You're not from around here, are you?"

"No sir, I'm not. I'm from Hazard, up in Perry County."

"Well, sir, the best place I know is Mrs. McQuinn's place. Mrs. Catherine McQuinn has always got a bottle to sell, and if you want some, uh, female companionship, if you know what I mean, she can help you there too. Just go back down the road a piece and her house is the first one on your right. You can't miss it."

Tom smiled at the young man. "Much obliged." Turning the horse around, he rode back down the road to Mrs. Catherine McQuinn's house.

Chapter 12

Quicksand

Catherine McQuinn's house was located near the mouth of Smith's Branch on the South Fork of Quicksand Creek. The house was a small one-story structure, painted white with black shutters and surrounded by a white picket fence. Rose bushes grew in the front yard. Mrs. McQuinn's cottage didn't look like a house of ill repute. A barn and outhouse were located in back. Tom tied his horse to a hitching post, then knocked on the door. A tall woman with a manly—almost athletic—appearance answered the door. Mrs. McQuinn's hair was as black as coal. Her wide-set, dark gray eyes appeared to support a high forehead, crudely balanced by large lips and a large, prominent nose. She instantly recognized Tom's name and welcomed him to board with her as long as he liked.

Tom had planned to stay only a night or two, but he enjoyed living on Quicksand Creek. And there was plenty of whiskey! He stayed at the house for several days before beginning a sexual relationship with the forty-six-year-old Mrs. McQuinn.

McQuinn's husband, Jeremiah, was a Confederate Veteran of the Civil War. Jeremiah was now a patient at the Eastern Kentucky Lunatic Asylum, in Lexington. He was institutionalized after developing mental problems upon the discovery that his wife was having an affair with a man who worked for the Day Brothers' Store in nearby Jackson. After learning that his affair with Mrs. McQuinn had turned her husband into a mental case, her lover in Jackson took his own life.

The South Fork of Quicksand Creek was about four miles from Jackson. The North Fork of the Kentucky River has several unusual bends within Jackson. The river swings around a great loop for nearly seven miles and comes back to within sixty-eight feet of itself. The top of an intervening ridge is known as the Pan Handle. It is about 150 feet above the water and so narrow that only one person can walk along it. Then it widens out into what is known as Pan Bowl Lake.

Tom visited Jackson often. One September afternoon, he drank so much moonshine that he became intoxicated. Next, Tom began to try to run the town. He and several of his new friends began shooting at Town Marshall H.C. Hurst, Jr. and his deputy, Samuel Mans. The lawmen returned fire. Mans hit Smith in the left arm, shattering the bone into splinters. For all his violent exploits, it was Tom's first serious wound. He returned to Mrs. McQuinn's house to recuperate.

One night Tom and Cattie—as she liked to be called—were in bed when Tom had one of his fits. It nearly scared Cattie to death. "Tom, what in the world is wrong with you?" When he finally calmed down after howling, falling onto the floor, gagging, and nearly swallowing his tongue, Tom told her that he had been bothered from time to time with these fits, and no one had been able to help him.

Cattie said, "There's a doctor in Jackson that might be able to help you. His name is John Rader. Although it doesn't do him much good, Doc comes around here sometimes because he likes one of the house-keeping girls, Louise Southwood. In the spring, summer, and fall, Louise stays here from time to time, tending to my garden. She is the best gardener thar ever was."

"Fine, I'm going into Jackson today," Tom said. "I'll ask him to come out and stay the night so he can be here in case I have another fit."

When Tom found Dr. Rader in Jackson, he said, "Doc, I've had problems with what people call fits since I was fourteen years old. I was wondering if I could talk you into coming out to Catherine's house at Quicksand and spending the night in order to check my symptoms."

Dr. Rader replied, "I've been wanting to court Louise Southwood, and I want you to help me do it. She's a pretty young thing, about sixteen years old. If you can get Mrs. McQuinn to make sure Louise is there, I'll do it."

"I'll make sure she is there."

Dr. Rader was one of four physicians in Breathitt County. However, Dr. Rader had a checkered past according to an article written on February 8, 1895 in the *Jackson Hustler*, the local newspaper of the day. After shooting and wounding John Hurst at a grocery store that Hurst owned in Lexington, Rader was given prison time. According to testimony at Dr. Rader's trial, John Hurst shot and killed Dr. Rader's brother over a disputed line fence and was sentenced to seventeen years in prison for the crime. After serving only three or four years, Hurst was pardoned by the governor. After Hurst was released from prison, he set up a grocery store in Lexington. Dr. Rader had threatened revenge for his brother's death. About dark one evening, Hurst was shot while sitting in the open door of his store. Hurst was shot five times by someone hiding behind an object. Hurst claimed he saw the shooter and that it was Rader. The physician was arrested and quickly convicted of the crime. He was sentenced to two years in prison, but served only eighteen months. He had been released from prison about eighteen months before coming to Jackson.

After serving part of his sentence, Rader was pardoned by Governor John Y. Brown. At that time there was no parole system in Kentucky.

Chapter 13

The Murder of Dr. Rader

Rader arrived at the McQuinn house, bringing along a gallon jug of whiskey. Louise Southwood was there doing some housework, but she ran away when Rader tried to get her to go to bed with him. The physician ran after the teenager, caught her, and briefly forced her back into the residence. Catherine McQuinn, Dr. Rader, Tom Smith, and neighbor Bob Fields—a teenager—were the only people in the house later that night. Soon Smith passed out drunk. Mrs. McQuinn and Fields took Bad Tom's shoes off and put him into a bed. All four slept in the same room.

The next morning Dr. Rader was found dead in bed, still in bed clothes. He had been shot twice below the fifth rib on the left side, with the bullets passing through at the sixth rib on the right side. Powder marks on the bedding indicated he had been asleep when killed. The doctor left behind a wife and three children.

Breathitt County Sheriff Breck Combs came to the murder scene. Mrs. McQuinn told him she had shot Dr. Rader because he had made indecent proposals to her. She was arrested, along with Tom Smith. Sheriff Combs took him into custody because he did not believe Mrs. McQuinn. Many people thought there should be a coroner's inquest, but that was rarely done in the mountains of Kentucky.

Rumors began to float around. Some people even speculated that John Hurst had Dr. Rader killed in retaliation for the earlier shooting incident in Lexington.

Sheriff Combs, Tom Smith's second cousin, questioned him. Tom said, "Breck, Dr. Rader pulled out a pistol and showed it to me. The drunker the doctor got, the nastier he became." Tom said that Mrs. McQuinn told him Rader had threatened to shoot him before the night was over. When he was shot, Rader—like Tom—was passed out drunk.

Sheriff Combs took both Catherine McQuinn and Tom Smith to the county jail in Jackson. While incarcerated, Bad Tom sometimes had fits and woke up the entire jail. Tom had always liked to sing and while in jail he would sing for a group of reporters. Most of the time he would sing one of his own compositions.

Breathitt County was known throughout the state of Kentucky as "Bloody Breathitt" because of its history of violence. The county's residents wanted to send a message to the rest of the state that they would not tolerate the murder of a prominent physician. They wanted to make an example of Tom Smith. The fact that he had acquired a regional reputation as a "bad" man did not help his case. Also, Dr. Rader's friends and family demanded that Smith be tried and sentenced to death.

Chapter 14

Two Trials

Tom Smith's trial was held at the Breathitt County Courthouse in Jackson. Colonel Tom Howard, Commonwealth Attorney of Salyersville, prosecuted the case. The courtroom was packed with spectators. Howard had a very powerful and persuasive voice. Mrs. McQuinn refused to testify against Bad Tom. Howard asked for the death penalty. After hearing several witnesses, Jackson County Circuit Court Judge B.D. Redwine gave his instructions to the jury, and they left the courtroom to deliberate. Immediately, the jury began deliberating and came back after only three minutes! The verdict was guilty with a recommendation of death by hanging.

In passing sentence on the prisoner, Judge Redwine told Bad Tom, "The Grand Jury of Breathitt County returned in this court an indictment against you charging you with the crime of murder, to which indictment you waived arraignment, and pleaded not guilty. A jury was selected that was acceptable to both you and the Commonwealth to try the issue, who after hearing the evidence, the instructions of the court, and the argument of counsel, returned a verdict finding you guilty of murder, and fixing your punishment at death. Have you any legal cause to show why judgment should not be pronounced against you?"

Bad Tom answered, "No."

Judge Redwine continued, "The duty that is before me now is the most serious that the law requires at my hands, and is not surpassed by any that I have been called upon to discharge. It's an awful thing to take a human life, to say that a human being shall die, even when justice requires it, and the mandate of the law forces those entrusted with its execution to pronounce the sentence into the presence of its creator. It is a duty that jurors and officers perform with regret and which they would shun if it were not impelled by their oaths and by public necessity to punish crime. They are sustained in the performance of their duty in the reflection that they do this not for vengeance upon the guilty, the wicked, and innocent. But it is a duty which no man when called upon has either a legal or moral regret to shirk. It should in every instance be performed with a nerve and courage that will strike terror to the heart of every wicked assassin or red-handed murderer who would by violence undertake to avenge his real or imagined grievance. The scenes that bring you to this tragic accusation are too fresh for me to recount. If we permitted you to live a thousand years, you could never forget the dark and bloody crime that robbed Dr. Rader of his life.

"When you and your associates in crime hurried him into the presence of his creator without a moment's warning, and so far as the evidence shows, without justifying or the least excuse, you forfeited your right to live in a community that owed to you equal protection under the law. This seems to be the legitimate result of such a life as the evidence shows that you have lived. When men convert themselves into walking arsenals, fill themselves with liquid fires that destroy mind and conscience, and, defying the laws of God and man, bathe their hands in their fellow's blood, they should expect that the vengeance of the broken and violated law cry out against them, for it has been written that bloody and deceitful men shall not live out half their days. Your courage seems to be with you even now in this most trying moment. But you should seek a courage that would lead you to do right, to confess your crimes and acknowledge the truth. No other courage is worth possessing. The influences that surround your early life may in large measure be responsible for your misfortune. Being reared in a community where crime is rarely punished, associating with bad men, and following pursuits that tend only toward evil, may all have contributed to bring you to this sad end. It is a source of regret to me that Breathitt County juries have in the past shown too much leniency toward crimes like the one you are to suffer. But if I may express one opinion, I believe the time has come in Breathitt County when society will protect itself, when murder will be punished by the highest and severest penalty known to the law. The history of all civilized countries shows that where crime is punished with unerring certainty, it gradually diminishes and peace and good order prevail. I do not undertake to say what may be the final result, but judging from all of the circumstances that surround you and your crime, I feel like admonishing you to appear before the court that makes no mistakes and from which there is no appeal. If you have not disclosed the whole truth about this bloody crime, if anyone had any part in it, or influenced you in any way to do the terrible deed, you owe to society, to yourself, and to your God to tell the whole truth and let justice be done to all who had a part in this murder. You cannot afford to go into the presence of God with a lie upon your lips. Friends cannot help you now, foes cannot harm you now. There is one person only who has the power to pardon you here, and that is the Governor of Kentucky. What he may do, I do not know. But I urge you to look to another and higher power for a pardon. Men may commit crimes and escape punishment for a while, but from the vengeance of the divine law there is no escape. It is to be hoped that you may throw yourself upon the mercy of an old wise God and that you may receive His pardon. It is the judgment of the court that you be taken by the Sheriff of Breathitt County on the 31st day of May, 1895, between sunrise and sunset, and hanged by the neck until you are dead."

Catherine McQuinn was the second of the two to go to trial. Taking the stand in her own defense, the testimony was quite different from what she had told Sheriff Combs right after the homicide. This time McQuinn claimed that Tom Smith shot and killed Dr. Rader. According to Catherine, she was forced to tell authorities about doing the shooting herself or she would be killed. The woman added that Smith said, " I belong to a gang who have been sworn to avenge each other's wrongs."

Fult French of Winchester, Jesse Fields, Joe Adkins, and others were mentioned as Smith's companions in the "Perry County troubles" and as belonging to the gang. Tom Smith denied that he ever told Mrs. McQuinn anything of the sort, and insisted that the woman killed Rader. At the time of the murder, Smith claimed to be asleep. He was awakened from a drunken stupor by the shooting, and saw that Mrs. McQuinn was robbing Dr. Rader. Mrs. McQuinn was convicted of the charges against her and given a life in prison sentence.

A reporter from the *New York Herald* on May 12, 1895, interviewed Mrs. McQuinn at the Breathitt County Jail and wrote in an article, "Mrs. McQuinn is a woman of almost masculine appearance, being tall and apparently as strong as an Amazon. Her hair is nearly jet black, her eyes a dark gray, and her mouth very large and ugly. She, like nearly all mountain women, is a habitual smoker of tobacco. She is not worried and is sure her verdict will be overturned and she will get a new trial. She denies any complicity in the death of Dr. Rader." Catherine McQuinn's sentence was allegedly commuted after she spent over two years in the penitentiary, and she was set free.

Chapter 15

The Hanging

Bad Tom's escape attempt on May 26th had failed, but at least he was now in a cell at the Breathitt County Jail that did not have a window. Therefore, he did not have to look out and see the scaffolding that was being constructed for his hanging. June 28th at one o'clock in the afternoon was the date set for the execution.

During the days leading up to the hanging, Tom continued to have fits and would disturb the entire jail with screams and howls.

A few days before the execution date, newspaper reporters from all over the country, including John Fox, Jr. of *The New York Sun*, would visit the condemned man.

Sometimes Smith would sing songs that he had written. Fox, who at the time was well known, would become very famous by writing several best-selling novels, including *The Little Shepherd of Kingdom Come* and *The Trail of the Lonesome Pine*. Shortly after the hanging, Fox wrote a story about the execution that was published in *Harper's Weekly*. He was paid thirty dollars for it.

The song composed by Smith that he sang to Fox and the other reporters in jail the night before the hanging was:

I.

Don't Grieve After Me

I am going to walk through the Valley in peace

I am going to walk through the Valley in peace;

Oh! When I am dead and buried

In my cold, silent tomb,

I don't want you to grieve after me.

II.

I am going to lay down my life for the Lord

I am going to lay down my life for the Lord;

Oh! When I am dead and buried

In my cold, silent tomb,

I don't want you to grieve after me.

III.

I am going to leave all my friends in peace

I am going to leave all my friends in peace;

Oh! Oh! When I am dead and buried

In my cold, silent tomb,

I don't want you to grieve after me.

CHORUS:

I don't want you to grieve after me

I don't want you to grieve after me;

Oh! When I am dead and buried

In my cold, silent tomb,

I don't want you to grieve after me.

Written long before the scheduled execution, the song was most appropriate.

Fox had previously written stories about the public hangings of Talton Hall and Marshal Benton "Doc" Taylor at Gladesville, Virginia in Wise County near the Kentucky state line. Fox had a residence in the Wise County town of Big Stone Gap. Talt Hall was known as Bad Talt Hall. He was finally captured by sometime lawman Marshal Benton "Doc" Taylor after Hall killed his thirteenth person. Hall escaped but was captured again. Doc Taylor was later arrested for his involvement in the killing of four members of the Mullins family in Wise County. Hall and Taylor were put in adjoining cells in the Wise County Jail in Gladesville. Hall was awaiting execution and Taylor was awaiting trial. Taylor had studied medicine in Louisville, Kentucky and was also a sometime preacher. Fox attended Hall's hanging first, which occurred on September 2, 1892.

Doc Taylor's hanging was on October 27, 1893. Fox referred to Taylor as Red Fox in his novel *The Trail of the Lonesome Pine.*

Taylor was a very colorful character who is said to have preached his own funeral, which started in his cell and ended on the scaffold when the trap door gave way. When he walked out of his cell to the scaffold, Taylor was dressed in a suit of white—which his wife made from a linen tablecloth—and he had a brown derby hat on his head. Taylor had instructed his wife not to bury him for three days and on the third day he would be resurrected. Taylor's widow had him buried four days after the hanging. Taylor was buried in an unmarked grave inside the

Wise, Virginia cemetery. The location of the grave was discovered over a century after his hanging. Hazard, Kentucky native, Faron Sparkman, of the Ben Caudill Camp of The Sons of Confederate Veterans, says his organization put up a gravestone for Taylor. The stone suggests that Taylor was a member of the 13th Kentucky Cavalry of the Confederate States of America. Faron Sparkman is the General Manager of WSGS and WKIC Radio in Hazard, Kentucky. His late father, Ernest Sparkman, gave the author of this book his first teenage job in radio broadcasting in 1958.

The first two hangings that John Fox, Jr. had witnessed and reported on occurred in the Wise County, Virginia county seat of Gladesville, later renamed Wise. The distance between Fox's home at Big Stone Gap and what was then Gladesville was only sixteen miles. He had to travel much farther—ninety-six miles—for the Bad Tom Smith hanging in Jackson. There was no railroad service, so the trip had to be by horseback. Fox rode through Hazard, where all of Bad Tom's murders, except the one he was to be hanged for, occurred.

In Jackson, Bad Tom's second cousin, Breathitt County Sheriff Breck Combs, told Fox and the other reporters, in no uncertain terms, who was in charge of the upcoming hanging, including its exact timing. Upon his return from a train trip to Frankfort and Lexington, Sheriff Combs told the assembled reporters, "I was down there to see the governor about that this morning and he was sorter of the opinion that it had best be done right about sunrise, because if it was put off the crowd would be bigger and there'd more likely be trouble. I kinder insinuated to him that a fellow ought to live as long as the law allows and it would be fair to all sides to split the difference and let him die twixt twelve and one. Anyhow, I can hang him when I please. It's me that's got the say now, but I thought as if he's the highest chief, I'd let him think about it. There won't be any trouble hanging him unless some fellow takes a notion to shoot him off the gallows. The only time there's going to be trouble is when Smith is dead and the roughs from the upper counties get drunk, and there'll surely be some shooting.

"I'm might afraid I'm going to have trouble getting the right kind of rope. I telegraphed to Louisville for a rope but the jailer didn't have any, and today when I was in Lexington, I didn't have any time to see about it. I can't get anything but an inch rope here and I don't want to hang the poor fellow with that kind of stuff. He ought to at least have a decent rope. I don't know about that roof. I don't know as if I'll put it on or not. Anyhow, it's nobody's business if I do. I'm running this thing, and I'm going to do as I please about it." The next morning, Sheriff Combs received a shipment by train of the type of rope he was seeking; it came from a hardware store in the west end of Louisville.

Tom did not sleep very well the night before the hanging. Sheriff Combs woke him at 5:30 AM. The sheriff admitted Tom's brother Bill and his sister Millie, after having them searched thoroughly. The family talked. Tom told them, "I want to make a confession of all my crimes."

Millie said, "Tom, don't do that until you get up on the scaffold."

"As soon as the telegraph office opens, I'm sending a telegram to Governor John Y. Brown asking for a stay of execution," Bill said.

Bad Tom received his last meal in his cell at six in the morning. It consisted of fried chicken, vegetables, bread, butter, milk, and coffee. Smith told Sheriff Combs, "Breck, this is the best meal I've had in many a year." He ate for forty-five minutes.

Bad Tom had requested to be baptized and Sheriff Combs agreed to allow it. As soon as Smith finished his meal, the official baptismal party was allowed to enter the cell. The party consisted of Smith's uncle, Reverend Thomas Kelly, an Old Regular Baptist minister, Reverend J.J. Dickey, a Methodist, and Reverend Stephen Carpenter of the Jackson Baptist Church. Reverend Dickey was also the editor of Jackson's only newspaper, the *Jackson Hustler*. The small group talked to Bad Tom for about fifteen minutes. The men marched Smith to the nearby North Fork of the Kentucky River, guarded by the sheriff and twenty armed men.

People began arriving on the day before the hanging. Many traveled long distances from Perry, Lee, Knott, Floyd, Magoffin, Wolfe, Owsley, Letcher, Rowan, and several other counties. They came on horseback, in wagons, and in buggies. Several arrived on foot, some barefooted. Most of the women wore sunbonnets. Many pitched tents on the river bank.

Excursion trains from Lexington and Cincinnati brought many people to the hanging. The special passenger train from Lexington began with only one traveler, a newspaper reporter. During stops in the mountain towns, people began boarding the train, and by the time it reached the train station across the river from Jackson, every seat on the train was taken and there were people sitting in the aisle. Those that came in by train had to cross the North Fork of the Kentucky River by ferry because the train station was located in the community of Inverness.

When the baptismal march from the jail to the river began, sightseers joined the ministers, sheriff, and guards. Because so many people crowded around, the guards had to forcibly make a small path for the ministers and Smith. Bad Tom and the baptismal group walked to the river between two long lines of Winchester rifles. The group entered the river at the Jackson ferry crossing. When they got to the water, everyone looked at Smith. His face revealed little emotion. He said nothing and the crowd was silent. Reverend Carpenter broke the silence, announcing an upcoming prayer for Smith. He invited those related to Smith to come forward to pray with their kin for the last time. Nearly 300 men, women, and children came forward. Smith had his back to the river; relatives surrounded him on three sides. Reverend Carpenter gave a signal and the large group got on their knees. Carpenter prayed for a solid fifteen minutes. During the prayer, he asked God to forgive Smith for his bloody and dark crimes.

Smith had shown no emotion when he arrived at the river. However, during Reverend Carpenter's prayer he began to cry. Smith was not the only person in tears. Many people in the crowd wept. At the conclusion of the long prayer, Reverend Dickey began a baptismal song. Nearly the entire crowd joined in the singing. The song book used by the ministers at the baptism was a pre-Civil War Old Regular Baptist Sweet Songster owned by Reverend Kelly. The singing was so loud it could be heard at Quicksand, where the murder of Dr. Rader had occurred. The song was very long, and as each verse was sung, Smith appeared to grow more pale. When the singing was finished, all three officiating ministers grouped around Smith and led him out into the middle of the North Fork of the Kentucky River, where the water was waist high. Reverend Kelly asked Smith if he had repented of his sins and accepted Jesus Christ as his Savior. Smith replied, "Yes."

Reverend Kelley raised his hand in the air and said, "Thomas Smith, I now baptize you in the name of the Father, of the Son, and of the Holy Ghost." He dunked Smith under the water. When the prisoner came up, he was sputtering, apparently having swallowed some water. Tom faced the crowd, smiling. He was then led slowly from the river. Once on the riverbank, many people from the crowd rushed to shake hands with Bad Tom. Sheriff Combs allowed Smith to shake hands with them because this would be his last opportunity to talk to friends and family. Again the guard had to clear a path for Smith to be led back to the jail. A guard handed him a towel to dry himself. He also received a black suit, obtained from Hargis Brothers' store in Jackson.

Tom's spiritual advisor, sister Millie, and Jailer Centers listened to Smith sing several songs. He then delivered a long, fervent prayer, asking God's forgiveness for many crimes. When the time for the execution approached, Smith came up with an idea for trying to stop—or delay—the hanging. Tom asked Sheriff Combs for a pencil and a sheet of paper to scribble down some words.

He wrote, "I would like a few more days' time, as I am an orphan boy, and have no friends. Signed: Tom Smith."

Tom turned to his brother. "Bill, send this telegram to Governor John Y. Brown. Who knows, the governor might give me some more time."

"I will send the telegram right away," Bill said.

A crowd of about 5,000 people—about evenly split between men and women—had gathered around the scaffold. Fifty guards armed with rifles, shotguns, and pistols surrounded the scaffold so the people could not get within fifty feet of the structure. Some of the people expected trouble. Sheriff Breck Combs was known to be a second cousin and a close friend of Bad Tom Smith. Rumor had it that Combs had selected the fifty guards from among friends of the convicted man. Residents of Jackson formed an outer guard of 250 men to make sure that the hanging took place and that Bad Tom could not escape into the woods.

The previous day's train had carried about 100 gallons of whiskey to the Inverness station. However, the Lexington and Eastern Railroad authorities refused to deliver it and shipped it back to Lexington. The railroad rightly feared the threat of drunks with guns.

At 11:30 in the morning, Sheriff Combs decided to postpone the hanging. Smith told him he was having trouble finding forgiveness from God for having killed Dr. Rader. He said he needed more time. One of the deputies mounted the scaffold and loudly announced to those assembled, "The execution is postponed until one o'clock so the condemned can get his soul saved."

The crowd then began to disperse for lunch. Just before one o'clock, the crowd started to reassemble. Several men got on top of a nearby shed for a better view. The shed collapsed under their weight and six men were pitched to the ground. No one was seriously hurt. At 12:30 a telegram arrived, addressed to Bad Tom Smith. Sheriff Combs opened it and read the message to him.

"I must decline to interfere. Governor John Young Brown."

Smith turned pale. He said to Combs, "Well, I guess I have to go, but I want all the time on the scaffold you can give me." Sheriff Combs told Smith he could have all the time desired. After another prayer with the assembled preachers, Bad Tom announced he was ready to meet his fate.

At one o'clock, Smith climbed up the steps to the gallows, accompanied by the preachers, his sister Millie, and several reporters, including John Fox, Jr. Fox wrote in his article—published in *Harper's Weekly* shortly after the hanging—that Bad Tom was not what he expected. He did not look like a killer. "He was a good-looking fellow, just over thirty with a pallid face, a black mustache of the mountain dandy, black hair, and black upper and lower lashes that literally lay on his cheeks. The eye under them was blue, languid, and bold only when he looked into a woman's. Smith played the banjo and sang, and as he himself said, women would leave their husbands to follow him." Although the sun was very hot, Smith remained on the gallows for forty-five minutes. The preachers, his sister, and the reporters were there for half an hour.

After climbing the steps to the gallows, Tom Smith began his confession, with some of the reporters transcribing it. Bad Tom told of the men he had killed, including the first one, Joe Hurt, who had come to his house in Hazard. He had helped kill Joe Eversole and Nicholas Combs. His companion, Joe Adkins, fired a shotgun at Eversole and Combs. As the two fell from their horses, Tom shot them again. He robbed Eversole's body of thirty dollars. During the Battle of Hazard, Smith killed Jake McKnight. He and Jack Combs killed Robin Cornett while the victim was cutting logs. Smith also finally admitted to the killing of Dr. Rader. He said Rader was acting ugly that night. Mrs. McQuinn told Tom that if he didn't kill Rader, the doctor would kill him.

He added that McQuinn told him she would take the blame if he killed Rader. "Nobody told me to do it except her. I did not do it for money. She took what money Rader had out of his pocket, but I don't know how much it was." John Fox, Jr. said that, following the long confession, Bad Tom wiped his forehead, gave a deep sigh, and smiled as though a weight was at last gone.

Smith talked to Millie after the confession. She advised him to tell only the truth and added that he should try to meet his God like a man. Smith then looked out to the 5,000 people surrounding the scaffolding and, facing south, addressed them. "Friends, one and all, I want to talk to you a little before I die. My last words to you on earth are to take warning from my fate. Bad whiskey and bad women have brought me where I am. I hope you ladies will take no umbrage at this, for I told you the God's truth. To you, little children, who were the first to be blessed by Jesus, I give you this warning. Don't drink whiskey and don't do as I've done. I want everybody in this big crowd to not wish to do the things that I have done, and to put themselves in the place I now occupy, to hold up their hands." All the hands in the crowd went up. Bad Tom continued in his clear voice: "This is beautiful! It looks like what I shall see in Heaven. Again I say to you, take warning from my fate and live better lives than I have lived. I die with no hard feelings toward anybody. There ain't a soul in the world that I hate. I love everybody. Farewell, until we meet again."

He kissed his sister goodbye and she left the scaffold. Millie did not stay to watch the hanging. Instead, she went to the jail to await her brother's body. Bad Tom then knelt down on the trap door and prayed a long, fervent, hysterical prayer for ten minutes. After the prayer, Tom walked around the scaffold for several minutes with the Reverend J.J. Dickey holding him on one side, and Detective George Drake supporting him on the other. The three made five or six turns around the platform.

Smith asked the ministers who were there to sing another song. They asked which one, and he replied, "How about *Guide Me, Oh Great Jehovah*?" The men sang the song and Smith knelt down to say a prayer. Sheriff Combs told him it was time, but Bad Tom asked for another song called *Near the Cross*. The preachers sang the song but the crowd did not join in this time.

Sheriff Combs put leather manacles on Smith's legs, then adjusted the noose. He placed a black cap over Smith's head, and drew the heavy white curtains on the scaffold around him. Those close to the gallows heard Smith say, "Save me, oh God, save me!" Next, the rope connected to the lever that held the trap door was cut with an ax by Sheriff Combs. Bad Tom's body fell six feet, snapping his neck. Although the white curtains concealed the tightening of the noose around Smith's neck from the crowd, it was obvious what had happened when the trap door was released. There was a scream of terror, and an answering wail by Millie, who was standing at the edge of the crowd just outside the jail. The Breathitt County Jailer's wife tried to comfort her.

Mrs. Armina Bowling Rader, the widow of murder victim Dr. John E. Rader, stood in the crowd with her brother and three small children. Dressed in black, she showed a curious smile throughout the proceedings. Someone in the crowd asked Mrs. Rader, "How air ye?"

She said, "I'm feeling mighty good now." She and her brother lifted the youngsters so they could observe the death of the man who killed their father.

Bad Tom's wife, whom he had left a little over a year before, was also in the crowd, dragging along her three youngest children—John, Cody, and Edgar. Emma sweated profusely. Already weary from dragging three young children around all day, she nearly fainted several times. When Emma saw people she knew, they looked away, either in horror or in pity. Her eldest child, Tildy, thirteen, was allowed to make her own decision about attending. She (the author's grandmother) chose not to.

It took seventeen minutes for Bad Tom Smith to be pronounced dead. Sheriff Combs asked for a sharp knife to cut the body down. One of his deputies, Bob Terry, handed him a two bladed Wade and Buchs brand knife to cut the rope. Smith's body was then handed over to his relatives, who prepared to take it some fifty miles to what is now Vicco for burial beside his mother and father.

Five months after the execution of Bad Tom Smith, in November, 1895, reporter W.L. Lampton came through Jackson. Everything appeared normal. However, he noticed that the scaffolding from which Bad Tom Smith was hanged was still standing. When he asked around, nobody would admit to knowing why that was.

Chapter 16

The Burial

A wagon pulled up to the scaffold and several men loaded the body of Bad Tom into a plain pine coffin and nailed down the lid. Tom's brother, Bill, told Millie it was over. The sister walked up and looked at the coffin briefly. They climbed onto the wagon for the long trip to the Jim Stacey residence at what is now Vicco near the Perry-Knott County line fifty miles away. Nearly 500 people accompanied the wagon and two-mule team. Most were relatives, but some were just curious. The journey lasted close to twenty-four hours, with only one stop for a few hours' sleep. On the stop in the Hardshell community near the Breathitt-Perry County line, a man at a nearby house said the body was beginning to smell bad. A woman living in a nearby house was Bad Tom's first cousin. Her father was a brother of Bad Tom's father, Richard Smith, Jr. The wagon finally reached the Jim Stacey homestead, with its nearby small graveyard, in the middle of the day.

The family transferred the body to a more expensive casket with a glass top over the face and chest. Those who attended the funeral service at the Stacey home could see Bad Tom's neck, badly stretched and purplish. Some said that this was the first glass-topped coffin used in the area. Most people were buried in homemade pine coffins similar to that in which Bad Tom was first placed. We do not know who paid for the expensive casket, or why he, she, or they would have selected a glass-topped model. There is some speculation that the benefactor might have hoped that others would see the fate that would befall them if they followed Bad Tom Smith's path. Some wonder if Susan Eversole purchased it, since she had the financial resources. Finally, the men of the family lowered Bad Tom's coffin, with his face looking up through the glass, into his grave.

Emaline Smith not only attended the hanging of her husband, but also made the fifty-mile journey to what is now the town of Vicco with his family, for the funeral which was held in the Jim Stacey house. Stacey was a close relative of Bad Tom. Susan Eversole, the widow of Joe Eversole, whom Bad Tom had murdered, also attended. Within the family, it is said that Emaline Smith and Susan Eversole, who were cousins, sat on the porch of the Stacey home following the funeral. They discussed how Emaline's six children would be taken care of. The following day Emaline and her children got aboard a wagon and rode to Hazard with Susan Eversole to her home. Mrs. Eversole agreed to help take care of Emaline and her children indefinitely.

The site of Bad Tom Smith's grave is not definitively known. He is believed to have been laid to rest in what is now the town of Vicco. At present, Vicco is a sixth-class city in Perry County, near the Knott County line. The city is located on Kentucky Highway 15 near the Carr's Fork Lake, which was formed from Carr's Fork of the North Fork of the Kentucky River, nearly twelve miles east southeast of

Hazard. The lake is now a Kentucky State Park.

There may have been a settlement at this location when Bad Tom Smith was buried in 1895. However, after his burial and the coming of the railroad to Perry County in 1912, the Montgomery Creek Coal Company was established in the vicinity. The community and the post office were both called Montago, after the coal company and the creek which joins Carr's Fork at this point. The Montago post office opened on March 1, 1921, with William McKinley Stacy as postmaster. The town was renamed Vicco in 1923 for the Virginia Iron Coal and Coke Company, which dominated coal production in the area.

The Vicco Baptist Church and the nearby Carr's Fork Lake were not in existence when Bad Tom Smith was buried in 1895. However, a Tom Smith who died in the 1920s was buried to the right of the back entrance of the Vicco Baptist Church. At the present time, the Vicco Baptist Church Cemetery contains a tombstone with the name of the outlaw "Bad Tom Smith." Seemingly, the new stone placed there in the 1990s is sitting on top of the original grave of a Tom Smith. Somehow, a mix-up has occurred.

Some people (including relatives) have long believed that is not the cemetery plot of the man hanged in Jackson, Kentucky in1895. Many now believe that another Tom Smith, a railroad worker, was originally buried in the Vicco Baptist Church Cemetery in the 1920s. Some say that the other Tom Smith was a teacher at one time. His original tombstone has disappeared, and in its place is a newer tombstone declaring that to be the burial site of outlaw Bad Tom Smith.

In the very late 1940s, several decades after Bad Tom Smith's death, four of his granddaughters (the author's aunts) and one grandson (the author's father) remember going to a primitive graveyard where Tom is buried alongside his parents and other family members. Therefore, some family sources now believe that the grave of Bad Tom is in a fenced grown-up patch of weeds on hillside land. Back then in the old Smith family cemetery, all of the old rocks used as tombstones were falling apart. The unmarked burial spot is straight down the hill, across three city streets, a railroad track, and Montgomery Creek from where a newer tombstone was placed at the Vicco Baptist Church Cemetery with the name Bad Tom Smith. All pictures taken of Tom's supposed tombstone are of the 1990s stone now on display.

According to other family members making a trip to Vicco in the 1990s, Bad Tom's grave is on isolated fenced farm land. Specifically, the land lays about an eighth of the way up the mountain from Montgomery Creek, which goes through Vicco. The downtown stores have a street running next to the creek. In the 1990s, a convenience store-type building was located on that hillside just above the creek. No other buildings were there. However, there was a fence to the left of the front of the store. The land on the other side of the fence is where the Smiths are supposed to be buried. The graves of Bad Tom Smith and his parents are thought to be way in the back of the land where a Methodist Church was once located. Jim Stacey's house once stood some distance away upon the opposite hill. Both structures are now gone. Stacey is said to have once owned most of what is now Vicco.

Epilogue

The French-Eversole Feud reportedly claimed the lives of about seventy-four people over a period of seven years. According to some sources, it was actually a feud within a feud, originating in the Civil War, when a member of the pro-Confederate Gambrill family was killed by an Eversole, who supported the Union. It is said to have been the most expensive of the mountain feuds in Kentucky. The dispute cost both Fult French and Joe Eversole in excess of one hundred and fifty thousand dollars to maintain their armies, not to mention costing Joe Eversole, and ultimately Fult French, their lives.

Bad Tom Smith's confession on the scaffold implicated Fult French, Jesse Fields, and Joe Adkins in the murder of one of the victims, Judge Josiah Combs. Tom confessed that he was present at the home of Jesse Fields on Buckhorn Creek, in Breathitt County, when the assassination was planned. Bad Tom claimed not to have had anything to do with the killing because he was recovering from a bullet wound in the arm inflicted by Jackson Deputy Town Marshall Samuel Mans. French, who had denied having anything to do with the murder, was indicted following Smith's confession.

Some people claimed that Bad Tom lied about not being involved in the judge's murder, but others reasonably argued that Smith had no reason to lie about French's complicity in the assassination, then to tell the truth about the murders he did commit. Fult French was acquitted following the indictment. Jesse Fields and Joe Adkins were also indicted. Both received life sentences for the murder of Judge Josiah Combs. They were defended by the man many considered the best lawyer in the state of Kentucky, William Campbell Preston Breckinridge. Breckinridge had served several terms as a U.S. Congressman from Kentucky. Not only well known in Kentucky, he was nationally renowned as a lawyer and an orator. He was also a first cousin of former Vice President John Breckinridge.

William Breckinridge won reversal of their cases on appeal. In a second trial, Adkins received a life sentence and Fields was acquitted. Adkins served eight years, then was pardoned. Following his release, Adkins left not only Kentucky, but the United States.

Catherine McQuinn served only two years of her life sentence. During her incarceration, McQuinn's husband, Jeremiah McQuinn, died in the Eastern Kentucky Lunatic Asylum in Lexington. She could not go back to the home on the South Fork of Quicksand Creek because her former father-in-law, Charles McQuinn, had claimed her property. In a lawsuit, Charles argued that his son, Jeremiah, was not of sound mind when he signed papers turning the ownership of the property over to his wife. The court concurred and awarded him the property.

After her release from prison, Mrs. McQuinn went back to Breathitt County briefly, then left the state of Kentucky. On April 1, 1907, Catherine Allen McQuinn is shown applying for a land grant in Harrison, Arkansas. In the 1910 census, she is found living as a lodger in Casa, Arkansas, and being of low income.

Catherine's father is recorded as living next door with his daughter, Martha Babe Allen Cowan, along with her husband and children. Joseph Allen died on July 25, 1911, at eighty-nine. He is buried in the Casa Cemetery in Casa, Arkansas. Catherine died on December 6, 1911, and is buried beside her father, Joseph Allen. The inscription on her grave marker reads, "Though Lost to Sight, to Memory Dear." Catherine was sixty-four years old. The cause of her death is not known.

Following the feud, Ballard Fulton French moved to Lost Creek, in Breathitt County, where he operated a general store for a short period of time. He moved on to Winchester, Kentucky, where he became a judge and opened a store. Those not connected with either side of the feud say that French never fired a gun, yet he obliterated the other faction and emerged from the feud unscathed and prosperous. His friends described him as a lawyer, merchant, and trader who was shrewd, genial, and most kindly. However, French knew he had made many enemies. He feared retaliation and began wearing a bulletproof vest.

In 1913, several years after the feud had ended and Bad Tom Smith had been hanged, French met Joe Eversole's widow, Susan Eversole, in the lobby of a hotel in Elkatawa, Kentucky, near Jackson. Mrs. Eversole wore black, even though it had been twenty-five years since her husband's death. She was accompanied by her son, Harrison "Harry" Eversole. At twenty-eight, he was a small man and possessed only one arm. Harry had accidentally shot himself in the hand some years ago, at eight years of age, and had to have his arm amputated. When French spoke to Mrs. Eversole, Harry pulled out a revolver and—aware that French wore a bulletproof vest—shot him in the spleen. French initially recovered from his wounds. The court fined Harry Eversole seventy-five dollars for disturbing the peace. His mother paid the fine. In 1915, a little over a year after the shooting, French died of complications from the wound. He is buried in Clark County at the Winchester Cemetery.

Harry Eversole was never tried for French's death. He died in Fayette County, Kentucky in 1939, at the age of fifty-three. His mother Susan died in Hazard in 1946, at the age of ninety-two. She is buried on Cemetery Hill in Hazard, where her husband, Joe Eversole, and her father, Josiah Combs, were laid to rest.

Emaline Smith was destitute in the fall of 1893 when her husband, Bad Tom Smith, left her with five children to raise, and pregnant with another child. Their sixth child, Edgar, was born after Tom went to Breathitt County.

Judge Josiah Combs and his wife Polly Ann Mattingly Combs moved to Barboursville during the trial of Fult French for the murders of Joe Eversole and Nicholas Combs. Then Judge Combs's wife moved back to Hazard from Barboursville. She was accidentally shot to death by her cousin in 1888, a few years before the assassination of Judge Combs.

Bad Tom Smith's so-called "fits" were believed to be grand mal seizures, today known as tonic-clonic seizures. They are associated with epilepsy.

Bad Tom Smith loved to sing and write songs. The only song that he is known to have written for a certainty is the one he sang the day before the hanging, *Don't Grieve After Me*. It survived because reporters transcribed it. Bad Tom wrote many other songs that did not survive. The song Emaline contained in the story was actually written by myself.

Some members of the family believe Bad Tom Smith wrote *Man of Constant Sorrow*. This classic first appeared in a song book published by Richard Burnett in 1913. Burnett said he did not write the song, but included it because he heard it somewhere and liked the sound. The songwriter is unknown, but immediate members of Bad Tom Smith's family remember *Man of Constant Sorrow* being sung around the house long before it was made popular by the Stanley Brothers in the 1950s, and years later in 2000 by the Soggy Bottom Boys in the motion picture, *O Brother, Where Art Thou?* The song has been recorded in various versions by numerous artists including Bob Dylan and Joan Baez, who did *Girl of Constant Sorrow*. Dick Burnett, a partially blind fiddler from Kentucky, first recorded the song. It is similar in style to *Don't Grieve After Me* and it is the type of song that Bad Tom would have written.

Bad Tom also played the banjo. It is not generally known that African-American musicians played an important role in developing instrumental Appalachian music by introducing the banjo in the late 1700s. The banjo became one of the symbols of mountain music. People in Appalachia referred to it as a "banjur."

Dr. Dan F. Hamilton of Leslie County, a character in this story, was the great-grandfather of my wife. During the French-Eversole Feud, Hamilton was a contemporary of Bad Tom Smith and practiced medicine in the area. The father of my wife was named after his grandfather, Dr. Dan F. Hamilton. Dr. Hamilton, who settled on Wooten's Creek in Leslie County, served not only the people of that county, but was a horseback-riding physician for several surrounding counties. He died in 1936 and is buried in the Hamilton Cemetery at Frew, Kentucky.

After Thomas Smith's execution, Sheriff William Henry Breckinridge Combs took part in only minor details of Breathitt County politics. Breck served in some capacity in every election. He was both an active and a founding member of the Masonic Lodge, in which he served as a Master Mason. Breck Combs died in the early morning of May 10, 1925 (almost thirty years after Bad Tom), in the front bedroom of his grandson, William "Jailer Willie" Combs's home in Jackson, from what was most likely pulmonary edema.

Jailer Willie's home hosted Methodist and Masonic services on the evening of May 11th. On May 12, 1925, Breck Combs was laid to rest with full Masonic Rites, beside his wife, Susan, in the Combs Family Cemetery on Hurst Lane, overlooking Snake Valley, in Jackson. He lies near thirty-two of his relatives and direct descendants.

According to the 1900 census, Tom's brother, Bill, and his wife, Sarah, moved from Leslie County to Knott County. The 1910 census found the couple living at Hazard in Perry County. Sarah Smith, who was older than Bill, died in 1917. Bill died in 1925, which is the same year that his sister-in-law, Emaline Combs Smith, died. Both

Bill and his wife, Sarah, are buried in the Bill Hill Cemetery near Jeff, Kentucky in Perry County. Reportedly in 1925, Emaline Combs Smith was killed by a car in Hazard, and is buried in the Hazard Cemetery.

Bad Tom's son, Bud Smith, remained a Presbyterian until his death in a mining accident at the White Jim Combs Coal Mine in Perry County in 1924. His older sister (my grandmother), Matilda Smith Combs, died in 1960. She is buried alongside her mother and brother, Bud, in the Hazard City Cemetery.

Ira Davidson, an Eversole faction member during the French-Eversole Feud, was Perry County Circuit Clerk for a number of years. He signed the marriage certificate for Tom and Emaline Smith in 1881. Davidson was one of numerous people run out of town by Bad Tom Smith and the French forces during the height of their power. Davidson was a half brother of Nicholas Combs, who was assassinated along with Joe Eversole by Bad Tom Smith and the French gang. Davidson took his two daughters, Malta Ellen and Annie Eliza, to London, Kentucky to live. His wife, Martha Combs Davidson, had died in childbirth. She was buried with her little baby daughter in her arms. Martha had asked her husband before she died to take the family and get away from all the killing. Shortly after he and his two daughters arrived in London, Kentucky, Davidson married Naomi Phipps. Even though he had moved to London, Kentucky, Davidson maintained his house in Hazard. When Davidson came back to Hazard in 1899, he discovered that his nephew, Frank Polly, had married and had moved Davidson's furniture out of Davidson's house to his own house. Polly, also a member of the Eversole faction, was described as the most daring and reckless of either faction. Davidson, upon learning that Polly had stolen his furniture, got into an argument with Polly and struck Polly over the head with a maul, killing him instantly. At the time, Polly was under indictment for complicity in the murder of Ed Campbell and Jake McKnight during the French-Eversole Feud. Davidson was a son-in-law of Judge Josiah Combs, a brother-in-law of Joe Eversole, and a half brother to Nicholas Combs, three of the men killed in the feud.

Dr. Rader's widow, Armina Bowling Rader, did not live long after her husband was killed and the man convicted of murdering him was hanged. Three years after Bad Tom's execution, Rader's widow, Armina, re-married. She wed Jackson County, Kentucky Judge Levi P. Johnston. A few months after the wedding in 1898, Armina decided to leave Judge Johnston and go back to her mother's home, where she had been living before the marriage. Judge Johnston, in a rage, pulled out a pistol and shot his wife to death, and then turned the gun on himself, dying instantly.

Bad Tom Smith's grandson (my father), Henry Clay Combs, was eighteen years old when his grandmother, Emaline Smith, died in Hazard. He was well acquainted with her. Combs lived the last thirty years of his life in Jackson, the town where his grandfather, Bad Tom Smith, was hanged. In the 1970s, he served a few years as Police Judge for the City of Jackson. In 1992, at age eighty-five, Henry died. He is buried in the Jackson City Cemetery.

Bob Fields, who was at the McQuinn house when the shooting

of Dr. Rader occurred, was only eighteen years of age at the time. He was a half great-uncle on my mother's side of the family. Fields was a step-son of my great-grandfather, Alfred Couch. He later served as Sheriff of Knott County for several years. Bob died in Hindman in 1965.

Jesse Fields, who—along with Joe Adkins and Boone Frazier—was accused of the assassination of Judge Josiah Combs, met an untimely end. On May 4, 1900, Fields was shot to death by his partner in the blind tiger business at Jackson. Fields and Adkins were indicted for the murder of Judge Combs and were tried in Barboursville. These proceedings ended in a hung jury. In a second trial, Fields was acquitted. Adkins was convicted and served several years in prison.

Tom Smith grew up without a father figure. His father, Richard Smith, Jr., was killed during the Civil War when Tom was only a toddler. Tom was ostracized in the community in which he was raised because of his epileptic fits. At the time, there was no medication to control his condition. Also, epilepsy was not well understood then. Even now it retains a social stigma. With all that going against him, one can understand some of the reasons Thomas Smith turned into what he became. However, even those issues do not excuse his becoming a thief, arsonist, and cold blooded killer.

It is ironic that Bad Tom's father, Richard Smith, Jr., was a soldier for the Union during the Civil War and was accidentally killed by his own troops. Tom worked for the French forces, many of whom had been supporters of the Confederacy. The French-Eversole Feud was, in a sense, a continuation of the feud between the Gambrills and the Eversoles that started during the Civil War.

One person demonstrated genuine Christian values during this sordid affair. Susan Eversole was putting a meal on the table for the pastor of her church when she learned that her husband, Joe, had been assassinated. Nevertheless, she assisted and supported her cousin, Emaline Smith, whose husband, Tom Smith, confessed to killing her husband. Joe Eversole left his wife in excellent financial condition. In true Christian fashion, Susan Eversole contributed part of her resources to help Emaline Smith, the widow of her husband's killer, and her children. Susan Eversole was truly a hero in this real life story.

Reverend Edward Guerrant and his teenage daughter, Grace, made a trip from Lexington to Hazard in 1896, a year after the hanging of Bad Tom Smith. They traveled by train to Inverness, and took a horse and buggy the thirty-five miles to Hazard. Grace Guerrant described the trip from Jackson to Hazard in a letter to her sister, Anne: "On Wednesday morning we started for the mountains in Perry County. We went up the Kentucky River ten miles to the mouth of Troublesome Creek. Here we got into trouble enough. We had to get out and help the buggy down the rocky stair steps in the road. We went up Troublesome about a mile, then up Lost Creek ten miles, then the man there said there were ten thousand big saw logs in the creek. I never saw the like. The little houses all had martin boxes but no yard or shade. Down on Troublesome, we saw some ladies barefooted, and one old lady had on shoes, but no stockings, and one had on a dress shorter than mine. I guess she must have been an old maid.

"The mountains were very steep, but had corn growing on their sides nearly to the top. They can't plow them up and down, but crossways. We saw coal mines all along the road, just sticking out of the mountains. Sometimes we rode over solid coal beds, and the biggest trees I ever saw grow along the creeks and rivers. They are awfully big. We saw a big boy who had only a shirt on, and most of the men were barefooted, but they were very clever.

"When we went ten miles up Lost Creek, we turned up a creek called 'Ten Mile Creek.' Well it was awful. I thought we had passed bad roads, but we were just beginning them. Three men went out along to cut trees and roll rocks out of the road. And such a road! Over big rocks and logs and steep banks and deep holes and around splash dams. I thought our buggy would be smashed all to pieces. The horse pulled our trace in two, and a big rock broke a spoke out of the buggy. Sometimes I bumped papa and sometimes papa bumped me. It was too funny. Papa got a man to lead a horse around a big tree on the mountain while he and another man held the buggy. The horse got strangled and the man cried out, 'Here's a dead horse,' and scared me nearly to death. But they got the horse up and we went over a mountain to the Grapevine Creek. Here we had a time getting down the mountain, the path was so steep and sidelong. Mr. Little's horse went over the mountainside and he jerked him back and he fell down, with the buggy on him. Papa and some men helped to take him out, then the buggy got away and ran down the mountain and broke the shaft. They all took our horse out and got the buggy down to the foot of the mountain by the hardest of work.

"The road down the Grapevine was no road at all. Mr. Little and Papa had to walk and lead and roll logs out of the way. It took us five hours to go seven miles. Mr. Sawyer, our missionary, was there. Papa is preaching in the little schoolhouse on the bank of the river, and it is crowded at 10 AM and 4 PM. Miss Kate Patrick and I play the little organ, the first one ever played in this county for worship. Emma Johnson has the only one in the county. The people are very clever and attentive, and most of them walk to church. About twenty-five have joined, and Mr. Johnson was the first one, and an old man nearly seventy, and a real pretty girl named Dora Duff. Mr. Johnson is the leading man in the county, and lives in the only brick house.

"Your sister, Grace."

The trip by the Guerrant party stopped in the small Perry County community at the mouth of Grapevine Creek. The word "clever" used in the Grace Guerrant letter to her sister is the mountain term for hospitable or generous. According to a second letter to her sister Anne, her father after preaching on Grapevine Creek for a few days continued their difficult journey over mountains and through creeks until they reached Big Creek, which is where Joe Eversole, the leader of the Eversole faction in the French-Eversole Feud, and his companion, Nicholas Combs, were assassinated by Bad Tom Smith and other members of the French forces a few years earlier.

Grace Guerrant said her papa preached at the schoolhouse on Big Creek for four days. Twenty-seven people joined the church. They then crossed the mountain to the community of Browns Fork, and then went over another mountain into the Perry County seat of

Hazard. While there, Guerrant and his daughter met with Emaline Smith, the widow of Bad Tom, her children, and Susan Eversole, the widow of Joe Eversole, one of Bad Tom's victims. They also checked on the progress of the First Presbyterian Church in Hazard, which Guerrant started with the help of Emaline and Tom Smith and others four years earlier. Today, the beautiful First Presbyterian Church of Hazard is one of the leading churches in the city.

Grace Guerrant, in a biography co-written with J. Gary McAllister—*Edward O. Guerrant: Apostle to the Southern Highlanders*—tells a story about a baptismal service her father held in Perry County. The minister was baptizing an old lady named "Aunt" Ferraby Noble, who insisted on immersion baptism. When he dunked her in Leatherwood Creek, she demanded to be dunked again, because, she said, the water in the creek was not deep enough. Guerrant, as a Presbyterian, did not believe in full immersion but in sprinkling. The immersion of "Aunt" Ferraby Noble indicated his sensitivity to the wishes of those he evangelized. Rev. Dr. Guerrant did not seem to have a problem with the lack of education of many Appalachian ministers. He supported and praised several mountain preachers with little or no education. Guerrant's problem was with ultra-Calvinism, the misquoting of scripture. One of the scriptures commonly quoted by many of the mountain clergy was from Romans 6:1 in the *New Testament*: "…continue in sin that grace may abound." The verse in context reads, "Shall we continue to sin that grace may abound? God forbid."

Rev. Dr. Guerrant had been a captain in the Confederate army, serving in Morgan's Command, during the Civil War. After the war he became a medical doctor, then entered the Presbyterian ministry. He was a native of Bath County, Kentucky, and a graduate of Centre College in Danville, Kentucky, Jefferson Medical College in Philadelphia, and Bellevue Medical College in New York. He attended Union Theological Seminary in Richmond, Virginia, but dropped out because of ill health. He later obtained a Doctor of Divinity degree from Austin College. Rev. Dr. Guerrant died in 1916 in Douglas, Georgia after an illness of one day, at the age of seventy-eight, while visiting his son, Dr. E.P. Guerrant. He is buried in the Lexington, Kentucky Cemetery. Rev. Dr. Guerrant founded more schools, colleges, orphanages, and hospitals than any other individual in Kentucky. He served as pastor of a Presbyterian church in Louisville, and then as an evangelist in the Kentucky mountain counties of Breathitt, Perry, Leslie, and Knott. In addition to founding the Hazard church, Guerrant also started a Presbyterian church in the Buckhorn community of Perry County and organized Stuart Robinson School, named after a prominent Louisville Presbyterian pastor. The Stuart Robinson School was originally a Presbyterian institution located in Blackey, in Letcher County.

Guerrant wrote several books, including *Bloody Breathitt*, published in 1890, *Forty Years Among the Highlanders* (1905), *The Galax Gatherers* (1910), and *The Gospel of the Lilies* (1912).

Joseph Eversole could have been an important man in Republican politics in the state of Kentucky had he desired and not been an early causality in the feud that bore his name. The national GOP convention Eversole attended failed to nominate incumbent Republican President Chester A. Arthur, and instead nominated former House Speaker

James G. Blaine of Maine for President and Senator John A. Logan of Illinois for Vice President. That ticket lost in the presidential election to Democrat Grover Cleveland of New York, who was elected President, and Thomas A. Hendricks became Vice President. Hendricks was the former governor of Indiana. The state of Kentucky cast its electoral votes for the Democratic ticket of Cleveland and Hendricks in the general election. Grover Cleveland is the only President in United States history to serve two non-consecutive terms. Republican Benjamin Harrison served between Cleveland's two White House stays.

Several book chapters and newspaper articles have detailed the French-Eversole Feud, or war, as it is sometimes called. Most of those paint Ballard Fulton French and his followers as the villains. They certainly were villains in the truest sense of the word. However, Joe Eversole and his followers were not entirely without blame.

It has commonly been reported that the dispute between Joe Eversole and Fult French started because Eversole became upset with French's legal representation of companies that were buying timber and mineral rights from fellow mountaineers at unfairly low prices. That may have been partly true. However, the real reason Eversole became fighting mad was most likely because a company French represented in court won a lawsuit against him, taking away land he considered his. Most people become angry when they personally lose something. Also, the Eversole faction was responsible for renewing the feud after Fult French and Joe Eversole signed a peace agreement on Big Creek. In addition, like the French side, the Eversoles used ambush techniques. There is plenty of guilt and blame to go around.

The French faction is often said to have won the feud. In reality no one won. The citizens of Hazard and Perry County were the real losers. Both the French and Eversole factions were fighting because of petty self-interests.

The Kentucky mountain feuds, including the French-Eversole Feud, made national news in the years following the Civil War. Newspaper reporters often wrote about the feuds as a product of ignorance, poverty, and isolation, and in some cases, inbreeding. However, most of the feuds, especially the French-Eversole Feud, involved educated lawyers and merchants and numerous followers fighting for local political power.

The population of Hazard was only about 150 at the start of the French-Eversole Feud. It declined to no more than seventy people during the fighting. After the Louisville and Nashville Railroad arrived in 1912, the town's population boomed. The railroad provided an economical means of hauling coal out of the mountains. The coal industry, still the major employer in the area, brought in jobs and people. Today, however, the coal industry in Appalachia is shrinking. The region once produced two thirds of the nation's coal. Coal mining employs only two percent of the Appalachian workforce. However, Hazard is now one of the major shopping and commercial areas for eastern Kentucky. Perry County overcame the disruptive lifestyle that the Civil War and the French-Eversole Feud brought to the Cumberland Mountains. Hazard is now a safe place to live, despite its name.

Sources

Kentucky's Famous Feuds and Tragedies, a book written by Charles G. Mutzenburg published in 1916 by R.F. Fenno and Co. New York, New York.

"Dr. Rader Murdered at Quicksand," an article in the *Jackson Hustler* published in Jackson, Kentucky on February 8, 1895.

"The Hanging of Bad Tom Smith," an article by John Fox, Jr. published in *Harper's Weekly* on August 10, 1895.

"Confessed on the Scaffold," an article in the *Louisville Courier-Journal* published in Louisville, Kentucky on June 28, 1895.

"Jackson, the Towniest Little Town of the Mountains," an article by W.J. Lampton in the *Louisville Courier-Journal* published in Louisville, Kentucky on November 8, 1895.

"Murder of Eight Men—Career of a Kentucky Outlaw About to be Hanged," an article in *The New York Sun* published in New York, New York on April 14, 1895.

"Beginning a Trial Which Involves the Perry County Vendetta," an article in *The Washington Post* published in Washington, D.C. on November 9, 1890.

"Flight After a Short Fight," an article in *The Washington Post* published in Washington, D.C. on December 11, 1894.

"Eastern Kentucky Anticipating Some Lively Shooting; Mountaineers Armed To Kill," an article in *The Washington Post* published in Washington, D.C. on December 12, 1894.

"French and Eversole; They and Ten of Their Followers Are Taken to Winchester, Ky. to be Tried for Murder," an article in the *Big Stone Post* published in Big Stone Gap, Virginia on September 5, 1890.

"The Cost of a Feud—The Leader of a Kentucky Vendetta Tells What It Costs Him to Protect His Life Maintaining an Army at $2,000 a Month," an article in the *Pittsburgh Dispatch* published in Pittsburgh, Pennsylvania on February 3, 1889.

"Prisoners of Perry—Sketches of Men Now in the Winchester Jail Awaiting Their Trial for Many Murders," an article in the *Big Stone Post* published in Big Stone Gap, Virginia on September 12, 1890.

John Fox, Jr., Appalachian Author, a book written by Bill York published in 2003 by McFarland Company Publishers, Jefferson, North Carolina.

Kentucky's Last Frontier, a book written by Henry P. Scalf originally published in 1966 and reprinted by The Overmountain Press, Johnson City, Tennessee in 2000.

Rugged Trails to Appalachia, a book written by Mary T. Brewer published in Viper, Kentucky in 1978.

The Hanging of Bad Tom Smith, a booklet written by Charles Hayes published in Jackson, Kentucky in 1969.

Trails into Cutshin Country, a book written by Sadie Wells Stidham published in Leslie County, Kentucky in 1978.

Trails and Tales of My People, a book written by Troy Baker Fields published in Hazard, Kentucky in 1999.

Night Comes to the Cumberlands, a book written by Harry M. Caudill published in Boston, Massachusetts by Atlantic-Little Brown in 1962.

Edward O. Guerrant: Apostle to the Southern Highlanders, a book written by J. Gary McAllister and Grace Guerrant published in Richmond, Virginia by Richmond Press in 1950.

Mountains, Moonshine & Memories, a book written by Donald D. (Dan) Caudill published in Bremen, Kentucky in 2004.

"Some of the Famous Vendettas of the Feud States; Mountaineers Who Carry On an Unending Warfare," an article written by Walter Q. Travistock published in the *Deseret Evening News* in Salt Lake City, Utah on May 30, 1903.

Newspaper archives from The Advocate Messenger, Danville, Kentucky, *The Winchester Sun*, Winchester, Kentucky, *The Jessamine Journal*, Nicholasville, Kentucky, and *The Intervener Journal*, Stanford, Kentucky.

"Catherine McQuinn Interview," an article in the New York *Herald* published in New York, New York on May 12, 1895.

That High Lonesome Sound, a filmed documentary about Appalachian music in Hazard and Perry County by John Cohen released in 1962.

Henry Clay Combs, grandson of Bad Tom Smith and the author's father.

Quentin Clay Combs, great-grandson of Bad Tom Smith and the author's brother.

Mary Ann Combs Browning, granddaughter of Bad Tom Smith and the author's aunt.

Nancy Combs Browning, granddaughter of Bad Tom Smith and the author's aunt.

Florence Combs Jones, granddaughter of Bad Tom Smith and the author's aunt.

Emma Combs Stout Hale, granddaughter of Bad Tom Smith and the author's aunt.

David Smith, President of Knott County (Kentucky) Historical, Incorporated in Hindman, Kentucky.

About the Author

Wayne Combs is a retired news broadcast journalist, minister, and college professor. He is a native of Hazard, Kentucky, and is a great-grandson of Bad Tom Smith. As a teenager, Combs began a broadcasting career in Hazard at WKIC Radio, now WSGS Radio. Although this is his first book, Combs has published several articles in national magazines. Combs earned an undergraduate degree in communications from Park University in Parkville, Missouri, as well as Master of Divinity and Doctor of Ministry degrees from Midwestern Baptist Theological Seminary in Kansas City, Missouri. Dr. Combs lives with his wife, Carol, in the Kansas City area. Both have been commissioned Kentucky Colonels. His daughter, Christin, lives in the greater St. Louis area.

www.ingramcontent.com/pod-product-compliance
Lightning Source LLC
Chambersburg PA
CBHW031954010726
47493CB00007B/2197